T. Evans, G. Villers Duke of Buckingham

The Works of His Grace George Villiers, duke of Buckingham

Vol. I

T. Evans, G. Villers Duke of Buckingham

The Works of His Grace George Villiers, duke of Buckingham
Vol. I

ISBN/EAN: 9783743401792

Manufactured in Europe, USA, Canada, Australia, Japa

Cover: Foto ©Andreas Hilbeck / pixelio.de

Manufactured and distributed by brebook publishing software (www.brebook.com)

T. Evans, G. Villers Duke of Buckingham

The Works of His Grace George Villiers, duke of Buckingham

V. I

T o

DAVID GARRICK, ESQ.

S I R,

THERE is a peculiar propriety in in-
scribing to you the works of *Villiers* Duke
of Buckingham, that zealous reformer of
the English stage; what his laughing and
poignant satire began, the justness of your
example has accomplished; and while sense
and nature adorn the writings of our dra-
matic authors, they are frequently height-
ened by your unrivalled excellence in
acting.

To you, Sir, the memory of the noble
Author has the greatest obligations; when-
ever your *inimitable performances of Bayes
and Don John delight the crouded theatre, his
fame is embalmed afresh*. His Grace was the
early friend and companion of a gay and

VOL. I.   a   dissipated

diffipated monarch; who, as a learned pre-
late remarks, took pride in corrupting the
morals of the rifing nobility; under fuch a
mafter, this accomplifhed nobleman purfued all the pleafures of a licentious and
abandoned court, from which the *graces*
fled.

Happy would he have been in his own
age, and revered by pofterity, if, like the
gentleman I now addrefs, he had united
real goodnefs of heart to great abilities.
That your health may long permit you to
entertain an admiring Public, and enjoy
the moft honourable connections, is the
ardent wifh of him who feels a ftrong fe-
licity in being able to boaft the friendfhip
of Mr. Garrick.

Strand,
May 1, 1775.

T. EVANS.

MEMOIRS

OF THE

AUTHOR.

THE noble Author, who is the subject of the following Memoirs, was son and heir of George Villiers, Duke of Buckingham, the minister and favourite of two sovereigns.

His Grace was born January 30, 1627, at Wallingford-House, in the parish of St. Martin's in the Fields, in the Liberty of Westminster, and baptized February 14, by Dr. Laud, then Bishop of Bath and Wells. The next year he had the great misfortune to lose his father by the cruel hand of an enthusiastic assassin, Lieutenant John Felton, who believing him the author of National Grievances, and too mighty grown for law, stabbed him at Portsmouth, August 23, 1628.

Charles I. endeavoured to console the Dutchess of Buckingham : he assured her he would be a husband to her, and a father to her children.

Her

Her Grace was then great with child, and being soon after delivered of a son at Chelfea, the King, and Francis, Earl of Rutland, the child's grandfather, were his fponfors. After fome compliments who fhould give the name, the King named him Francis; and the grandfather gave him his benediction of feven thoufand pounds a year.

The duke and his brother were bred up by the King with his own children, under the fame tutors and governors. Both the brothers were fent young to Trinity College, Cambridge, and their names entered in the college book with Prince Charles. Here the Duke became acquainted with the celebrated Mr. Abraham Cowley and Mr. Martin Clifford, for whom he ever entertained the greateft efteem: nor were they lefs attached to his grace. On leaving the univerfity, the duke and Lord Francis travelled abroad under the care of William Aylefbury, Efq. fon of Sir William Aylefbury, appointed to that office by the king.

They continued abroad till after the Civil War had commenced; and upon their return were conducted by their governor to his Majefty,

then

then at Oxford, where, as a teſtimony of their loyalty and gratitude, they aſſured the King of their firm reſolution to devote their lives and fortunes to his cauſe. Eager to give proofs of their zeal, they choſe Prince Rupert and Lord Gerrard for their military preceptors, acompany-ing thoſe noblemen into very deſperate ſervice, the ſtorming the Cloſe at Litchfield, in Stafford-ſhire; which Lord Clarendon remarks, was one of the ſharpeſt engagements that happened during the Civil War. The affection of the Dutcheſs alarmed her for the ſafety of her ſons : ſhe re-monſtrated with Lord Gerrard for tempting the youths into ſuch danger. He replied with the bluntneſs of a ſoldier : " It was their own incli-nation, and the more danger the more honour."

The parliament rewarded their valour by ſeiz-ing their eſtates, but with a compaſſion which does honour to that aſſembly, reſtored them, on conſideration of the youth of their noble foes.

The Dutcheſs of Buckingham ſoon after, by her imprudent marriage with the Marquis of Antrim, ruined herſelf, and offended her Sove-reign. Her ſons were committed to the care of the Earl of Northumberland, and went on their

travels

travels into France and Italy, but chiefly refided
at Florence or Rome, where they lived with the
fplendor of the princes of Italy.

They returned to England in the year 1648:
the war had proved unfavourable to their royal
protector; he was a prifoner in the Ifle of
Wight, feveral of his zealous friends determined
to hazard again the fortune of the field. Duke
Hamilton in Scotland; the Earl of Holland, and
others in Surrey, Goring in Kent, and many in
London and in Effex, appeared in arms.

The duke and his brother joined this laft
effort of the dying caufe; they repaired to the
Earl of Holland, and were the firft that took the
field, about Ryegate, in Surrey.

The parliament were perfectly acquainted
with thefe hoftile attempts, and defpifed them.
The infurrection growing formidable in Kent,
their General, Fairfax, received orders to march
and fupprefs them. That officer found a greater
oppofition than he expected, and met with a very
gallant refiftance, at the ftorming of Maidftone
and attack of Colchefter.

Colonel Gibbons marched againft the infur-
gents in Surrey: he obliged Lord Holland to
make

make a precipitate retreat to Kingfton, but over-
taking them at Nonfuch, gave them a total de-
feat, Lord Francis Villiers, at the head of his
troop, having his horfe flain under him, got to
an oak tree in the highway, about two miles
from Kingfton, where he ftood with his back
againft it, nobly defending himfelf, difdaining
to implore quarter, and the enemy barbaroufly
refufing to give it, and having received nine
wounds in his face and body, he expired.

The Duke of Buckingham, with great difficulty, efcaped to St. Neots, in Huntingdonfhire,
at which place the Earl of Holland arrived, who
was there taken, and foon after beheaded.

His grace finding the houfe where he lay fur-
rounded, and a troop of horfe drawn up before
the gate, muftered his followers, and charging
the enemy with determined refolution, intirely
routed them, killed their commanding officer,
and made his efcape to the fea-fide, and thence
to Prince Charles, who was in the Downs with
thofe fhips that had deferted the Earl of War-
wick.

The parliament, defirous to detach a nobleman of fuch rank and abilities from the Royal

caufe

caufe, offered him forty days to return to England. His Grace rejected thofe offers, and remained firm to the Prince.

His eftate was therefore a fecond time feized,
being, by the acquifition of his brother's,
which fell to him, the greateft of any fubject in
England.

The money he received for the fale of his pictures at Antwerp, was now his only fupport.
They were part of the coftly and curious collection of his father, procured from Italy by the
help of Sir Henry Wotton and others, and had
adorned York-Houfe, to the delight and admiration of all men of tafte *.

* This collection had been purchafed at great prices.
The late Duke gave ten thoufand pounds for what had
been collected by Sir Peter Paul Rubens; and Sir Henry
Wotton, when Ambaffador at Venice, purchafed many
other capital pieces for his Grace. After his affaffination, the King purchafed fome.——Others were bought by
the Earl of Northumberland and Abbot Montagu. A
judgment may, in fome meafure be formed, how valuable
the entire collection muft have been by the lift of what remained; where we find no lefs than nineteen by *Titian*;
feventeen by *Tintoret*; twenty-one by *Baffan*; two by
Julio Romano; two by *Georgioni*; thirteen by *Paul Vero-*
nefe;

These were secured and sent him by his old trusty servant Mr. *John Trayleman.*

nese; eight by *Palma*; three by *Guido*; thirteen by *Rubens*; three by *Leonardo da Vinci*; two by *Correggio*; and three by *Raphael D'Urbin*; beside several by other esteemed masters whose pieces are scarce.

Mr. Duart, of Antwerp, bought some; but the Arch Duke Leopold purchased the greater part, and added them to his noble Collection in the Castle of Prague. He bought the chief picture, the ECCE HOMO, by Titian, in which are introduced *the portraits* of the Pope, the Emperor Charles V. and Solyman the Magnificent; it is eight feet in length and twelve in breadth. Mr. Fairfax says it was valued at 500l. but from a note of the late Mr. George Vertue the Engraver, it appears, that Thomas, Earl of Arundel, offered the Duke's father the value of 7000l. in land or money *for this single piece.* The Duke also possessed another great curiosity in painting, *the stained glass window which now ornaments the east end of St. Margaret's Church, Westminster.* The magistrates of Dort, in Holland, being desirous of presenting Henry VII. with something worthy to adorn his magnificent chapel then building at Westminster, directed this window to be made, which was five years in finishing, King Henry and his Queen sending their pictures to Dort, from whence their portraits in the window are delineated. King Henry dying before the window was compleated, it became the property of an abbot of Waltham, who placed it in his abbey church,

where

The king refolving to go to Scotland, was attended by the Duke of Buckingham; and on their
arrival, when all the reft of his majefty's Englifh
fervants were removed, the Duke was alone ex-
cepted. The parliament again at this period
made overtures to the Duke, offering to com-
pound for his eftate at 20,000£. which was lefs

where it remained till the diffolution of the abbey by
Henry VIII. 1540; to preferve it from being deftroyed, it
was removed by Robert Fuller, the late abbot of Waltham,
to a private chapel at Newhall, an ancient feat belonging
to the Butlers, Earls of Ormond, in Wiltfhire, which afterwards became the property of Thomas Bollien, father of
Anna Bollien. In the reign of Queen Elizabeth, Newhall
was the feat of Thomas Ratcliff, Earl of Effex; from his
family, George Villiers, Duke of Buckingham bought it;
his fon fold it to General Monk. The general, to preferve this elegant window from the puritanical rage of his
own party, who had deftroyed above 800 beautiful win-
dows, ordered it to be buried. After the Reftoration, he
replaced it in the chapel of Newhall, which being afterwards the property of John Olmius, Efq. was by him de-
molifhed; the window was then purchafed by Mr. Conyers,
who paid Mr. Price, a great artift, a large fum of money
for repairing it. The fon of Mr. Conyers fold it to the
committee appointed for the repairing and beautifying
St. Margaret's, A. D .1758, for the fum of 400 guineas.

than

than a year's value; he rejected their offers, and determined to fhare the fortune of his fovereign, he marched with him from Scotland into England; during the march, perceiving very few of quality or diſtinction repaired to the royal army, he remonſtrated to the king, that it would be more for his majeſty's intereſt to remove the Scottiſh general, alledging it was not confiſtent with the honour of any peer of England to receive his orders, and folicited the king to confer on him that honour; his ſuit being rejected, the duke became ſo difcontented he came no more to council, fcarce ſpoke to the king, neglected every one and himſelf ſo much, that for many days he fcarce put on clean linen, ſhuning all converſation; in this *fullen diſpoſition he continued while the army remained at Worceſter; but in the battle there he was at the king's right hand, and behaved with exemplary valour.

The fuperior fortune of Cromwell prevailing, and the royal army being totally diſperſed, he retired northward with his majeſty, who had then an intention to retire to Scotland; but on a confultation with the Duke, the Earl of Derby,

Derby, the Lord Wilmot, &c. it was thought more convenient for his majesty to conceal himself in Boscobel House. The duke and other noble persons, with about sixty horse, having conducted the king to that place, and believing him in security, with great difficulty made his own escape into France, and went a volunteer to the French army, and signalizing his courage at the siege of Arras and Valenciennes, gained the esteem of the French officers.

He seldom attended the court of Charles; though the king was highly pleased with his company, and created him knight of the garter, but the courtiers and his grace were on bad terms.

During his residence in France he corresponded with his friends in England, they obtained leave from the government for his grace to return to his country, to which Charles also consented.

On his arrival he resolved by a bold stroke, (at the expence of his gratitude) to repair his fortune: he paid his court to the protector *, and solicited him to bestow on him one of his daughters in marriage. He treated the character of the king with raillery and contempt, as-

* Macpherson's Extracts from the Life of James II.

suring

furing the protector he defired nothing more than to venture his life againft Charles Stuart, as he then called him. This conduct did not fucceed, inftead of winning the favour of Cromwell it had the contrary effect. Cromwell replied, he would never give his daughter' to a man who could be fo ungrateful to the king, and who owed all he had to the Stuart family. Foiled in this attempt, he paid his addreffes to the daughter of Lord Fairfax; the parliament had beftowed on this nobleman part of the duke's eftate; with difficulty he fucceeded, and was married to Lord Fairfax's only daughter, a moft virtuous and amiable lady. Cromwell was much difpleafed when he heard of the match; he confented that the duke fhould refide at York Houfe with his family; but his grace going to Cobham to fee his fifter, he was committed to the Tower on the 24th of Auguft, 1658.

Lord Fairfax refented this treatment of his fon-in-law; he waited on the protector, and remonftrated fharply on his conduct to the duke in fuch terms, that Cromwell alfo grew warm, and turned abruptly from him, cocking his hat and throwing his cloak under his arm, as was

his

his cuftom when in a paffion. This was the laft meeting of Cromwell and Fairfax. On the death of the protector the duke had leave to be a prifoner at Windfor Caftle, where his friend Mr. Abraham Cowley was his conftant companion. At Windfor he remained till the 29th of July, 1659, when the abdication of Richard Cromwell reftored him his liberty, on his giving fecurity to be faithful to the government.

On quitting Windfor he retired to Lord Fairfax's feat at Appleton, in Yorkfhire, and here he fpent the happieft part of his life, becaufe the moft prudent, free from riot or extravagance. Lord Fairfax was highly delighted with his company, and rejoiced to fee him perfectly conformable to the order and good government of the family.

On the reftoration of Charles II. when the king formed his council at Canterbury, irritated with the duke for his paft conduct, he omitted his grace, who was the only man that had enjoyed that honour abroad that was not called to it at home. The charms of his wit and converfation had gained too great an afcendancy over the king for this mortification to laft long; he was

I foon

foon after made lord of the bedchamber and fwore of the privy council.

By his majefty's reftoration he regained his eftate, but his neceffities and expenfive living made him a prey to ufurers, which greatly impoverifhed his income. He lived at WallingfordHoufe in the utmoft fplendour, entertaining with great hofpitality the foreign nobility, efpecially the French, who engaged him in play, but he foon forfook the vice of gaming.

The favour of his fovereign did not attach him to the meafures of the court, he engaged deeply in oppofition, fet himfelf at the head of a party whofe counfel he folicited, lamenting the king's neglect of bufinefs, and his trufting to perfons totally incapable, exaggerating all the licentioufnefs and debauchery of the court in the moft lively colours; he was well qualified for fuch a narration, having himfelf been deeply engaged in thofe pleafures he now affected to difclaim.

He acquired a very great intereft in both Houfes of Parliament; his quality, his condefcenfion, the brilliancy of his wit, drew perfons of all affections and inclinations to like his com-

pany;

xvi MEMOIRS OF THE AUTHOR:

pany; even the moſt rigid believed, when the
vanities and levities of youth ſhould give place
to the ſoberneſs of age, he would be highly
uſeful to his country, for which he declared the
greateſt affection.

The king had conſtant intelligence of all his
conduct; he was highly irritated with him for
the freedom with which he treated his character,
and could ſcarce credit that the duke's levity and
love of pleaſure would permit him to attend to
parliamentary buſineſs, and acquire an incredible
opinion with the people.

The Duke of Buckingham made no ſcruple
of declaring his hatred againſt the Duke of Ormond, whoſe youngeſt ſon had married his
niece; he complained Ormond had violated
many promiſes of friendſhip, and reſolved to
ſeize every opportunity to diſtreſs him.

In the year 1666, a bill was paſſed for re-
ſtraining the importation of Iriſh cattle; an act
peculiarly hard, as Ireland had ſcarce any other
article for foreign commerce. The violence of
the country gentlemen, who aſcribed the ſudden
fall of their rents to the importation of provi-
ſions from abroad, overcame the king's ſolici-
tations,

citations, who declared he was equally king of all, and obliged to have an equal care of all, and never to confent to any thing that might be prejudicial to either of the others, efpecially if the benefit to the one was not proportionable to, and as evident as the damage was to the others; and upon thefe grounds, he recommended to them to give fuch a ftop to this bill, that it might never be prefented to him; he difcovered an inclination to refufe his affent, but was fwayed from his purpofe by his fears that the commons would give no fupply; during the debate, the Duke of Buckingham exerted all his talent for ridicule, to the great entertainment of the Lords; among other expreffions he remarked, that whoever was againft the bill had either an Irifh intereft or an Irifh underftanding.

This obfervation highly offended the Lord Offory (eldeft fon of the Duke of Ormond); confcious of his own impetuofity of temper, he declined an inftant reply, but meeting the duke after the debate, he defired he would walk in the next room, and there told him, " that he had " taken the liberty to ufe many loofe and un- " worthy expreffions, which reflected upon the

VOL. I.   b   whole

" whole Irish nation, and which he himself re-
" fented fo much, that he expected fatisfaction,
" and to find him with his fword in his hand."

In vain the duke urged the freedom of debate, Lord Offory was deaf to all accommoda-
tion; his grace therefore appointed in lefs than
an hour to decide this difference in Chelfea
Fields. Lord Offory inftantly repaired to the
place of combat; when, having waited fome
time, and feeing feveral perfons approach, he
concluded they were fent to prevent any action,
he therefore mounted his horfe and retired.

The duke was found by himfelf in another
place on the other fide of the water, which he
declared he imagined to be the place appointed.

The next day he took a refolution, from
which his friends diffuaded him; as foon as the
houfe of lords was fet, he told the houfe he muft
inform them of fomewhat that concerned himfelf, and being fure that it would come to their
notice fome other way, he had therefore chofen
to acquaint them with it himfelf; when having
related the caufe of the duel, he added, he had
told Lord Offory he would fight him, yet did
not think himfelf obliged to it in maintenance

of

of any thing he had faid or done in parliament, yet, that it being agreeable to him to fight with any man who had a mind to fight with him, he appointed Chelfea Fields, which he underftood to be the fields over againft Chelfea, that he only went to change his fword, and haftened to the place, where he waited in expectation of Lord Offory until fome gentlemen arrived, who declared they came to prevent his and Lord Offory's meeting; therefore, imagining there would not be any prefent combat, he had returned, but was always ready to give any gentleman fatisfaction that fhould require it of him.

The Lord Offory was much affected that the difpute was like to prove only a war of words. The houfe declared, a punifhment ought to be inflicted on Lord Offory, who had violated the freedom of debate, that the duke had conducted himfelf in this bufinefs according to the cuftom of the age, and had given no offence to the houfe, to which he had always paid a proper refpect.

Some lords declared, the duke by his readinefs to fight, had made the offence equal, and therefore moved they might both be fent to the tower.

The

The duke, who had often employed his talent for ridicule, was now doomed to feel the lafh himfelf; fome members defired his grace might receive no punifhment becaufe he had committed no fault, for it was evident that he never intended to fight, and had, when no other tergiverfation would ferve his turn, prudently miftaken the place that was appointed by himfelf; his friends thought this acquiefcence was efcaping too dear ; and therefore both lords were fent to the tower. The duke had no fooner regained his liberty, than he was engaged in a conteft with the Marquis of Dorchefter in a conference with the Commons on the Irifh bill, as his Grace and Lord Dorchefter were fitting in the Painted Chamber; they quarelled about their feats, and, in violation of all decorum, ftruck each other ; the houfe of lords committed them both to the Tower.

The king was highly incenfed againft the duke for his conduct in parliament this feffion ; and being informed the duke was plotting againft the government, he ordered him by proclamation to furrender himfelf; the duke foon found means to make his peace with the king, and was re-

ftored

ſtored to favour. The duke aſcribed his diſ-
grace to the Earl of Clarendon ; with all the
force of his poignant wit, he had long endeavoured to make that miniſter ridiculous in the
eyes of his ſovereign, he would frequently ſay to
the king, " There goes your ſchool-maſter."
He often acted and mimicked the chancellor before the king, walking ſtately with a pair of bel-
lows before him for the purſe, and Col. Titus
carrying a fire ſhovel on his ſhoulder for the
mace, to the great entertainment of Charles.
Above all, he promiſed for the conduct of the
commons ſhould his enemy be diſgraced. The
king ſoon abandoned the chancellor, who was
attacked by the commons, impeached and ba-
niſhed. On Clarendon's withdrawing, he left a
vindication of his conduct, addreſſed to the
lords ſpiritual and temporal in parliament aſ-
ſembled. The lords communicated this petition
to the commons, and at a conference between
the two houſes, the Duke of Buckingham delivered up the petition, and added by way of
inſult and deriſion, " That the lords had com-
" manded him to deliver to the commons that
" *ſcandalous and ſeditious paper,* ſent from the

" Earl

" Earl of Clarendon; they bid me prefent it to
" you, and defire you in convenient time to
" fend it to them again, for it has a ftile which
" they are *in love with, and they defire to keep it.*"

The cruelty of ridiculing the afflictions of a
great man, and the turning the juftice of the
nation into a jeft, offended the fober and the ferious, and they agreed with the earl when he
complained in his petition " of fome enemies of
" more licentious principles, who took to them-
" felves the liberty of reviling all counfels and
" counfellors, and turning all things ferious and
" facred into ridicule."

To prevent for ever the return of Clarendon,
Buckingham and Arlington endeavoured to an-
nihilate his party by difplacing his relations and
friends. In the month of May, 1668, he purchafed of the Duke of Albemarle the place of the
mafter of the horfe, and added the weight of an
oftenfible office to his fecret influence in the
cabinet.

Buckingham having triumphed over Clarendon and his friends, turned his whole influence
and policy againft the Duke of York, whom he
I   endeavoured

endeavoured in vain to difplace from his office of lord high admiral.

The whole life of his grace was ruled by caprice: purfued by meffengers and warrants in the month of March; in the Tower in June; in July leading the cabinet. He was now a firm affociate of that miniftry, whom the nation execrated, ftiling them in derifion, from the initials of their names, THE CABAL.

The Dutchefs of Orleans having been fent to meet the king, her brother, at Dover, to engage her to declare war againft the Dutch, on her return to France was fuppofed to be poifoned. The Duke of Buckingham appears to have been greatly affected by the death of the Dutchefs of Orleans; he profeffed a wonderful attachment to that princefs; he became outrageous on the news of her death; he talked of nothing but a breach with France; he flew to all the foreign ambaffadors, and without authority endeavoured to engage them in the expected war *. On the arrival of the Marquis of Bellesfond with compliments of condolance from the French king, Charles, who knew the character of Buckingham, fent him in return to France, infinuating

* Macpherfon's Hiftory.

at

at the fame time to Lewis, the propriety of gaining him to their fecret fchemes. The accefs to Buckingham was eafy through the channels of his vanity and avarice ; on his arrival Lewis affailed him through both. He remarked on his noble prefence and mien, adding, he was almoft the only *Englifh* gentleman he had ever feen ; greater refpect was paid him than was ever fhewn to any ambaffador ; a regale was prepared for him, worthy of the Roman emperors when Rome flourifhed in her utmoft grandeur. Lewis alfo prefented him with a fword and belt, fet with diamonds to the value of forty thoufand pi-ftoles. The Dutchefs of Orleans was forgot, and the duke entered heartily into the meafures of both fovereigns. -

The avowed enmity of the Dukes of Buck-ingham and Ormond made the former fufpected of being concerned this year, 1670, in the at-tempt of Blood againft the life of Ormond. The Earl of Offory foon after meeting Buckingham at court, ftanding by the king, his colour rofe, and he could not forbear expreffing himfelf to this purpofe, " My lord, I know well that you " are at the bottom of this late attempt upon

" my

" my father; but I give you warning, if by
" any means he come to a violent end, I fhall
" not be at a lofs to know the author; I fhall
" confider you as the affaffin, I fhall treat you
" as fuch ; and wherever I meet you I fhall
" piftol you, though you ftood behind the king's
" chair; and I tell you in his majefty's prefence,
" that you may be fure I fhall not fail of per-
" formance." Mr. Hume obferves, if there
was any indecorum in this fpeech, it was eafily
excufed. in a generous youth, when his father's
life was to be expofed to the dangerous attempts
of affaffins *.

While the duke took an active part in the political contefts of his country, he alfo endeavoured to augment her literary reputation; in his
travels he took particular notice of the decorum
of foreign theatres, efpecially the French, under

* If the Duke of Buckingham joined Colonel Blood in
the attempt againft Ormond, in 1680, Blood requited him
by fuborning evidences to fwear fodomy againft his grace.
The duke brought an action of *fcandalum magnatum*
againft this defperado, laying his damages at ten thoufand
pounds. This profecution threw Blood into an illnefs
which deprived him of his life.

the

the regulation of M. Corneille, then in its greateſt glory.

The Engliſh ſtage at this period exhibited ſcenes of lewd and ſenſeleſs jargon. The duke on all occaſions expreſſed his contempt and hatred of this fulſome *new* way of writing. He narrowly eſcaped with life from oppoſing the exhibition on the ſtage of the United Kingdoms ; the author having numerous friends in the houſe, ſome of them perceiving his grace heading a party who were very active in *damning* the play, by hiſſing and laughing immoderately at the ſtrange conduct of it ; ſome perſons were laid in wait for him as he came out, but he luckily eſcaped through the crowd ; he was afterwards hard threatened, but friends ſettled the matter amicably.

The duke reſolved however to expoſe to the people theſe *new-faſhioned plays,* and to exhibit in a clear light the traſh of which they were ſo fond. He therefore wrote the celebrated Rehearſal ; this play, as it is the beſt known of all our noble author's productions, ſo it has ever ſince been held in great repute, and eſteemed a piece of the moſt poignant ridicule and entertaining

taining banter. It is alledged that his grace
was affifted in writing this play by his chaplain
Dr. Thomas Sprat, Martin Clifford, Efq. mafter
of the charter-houfe, and Mr. Samuel Butler,
author of Hudibras. A confummate judge *
makes it a ftandard in the way of ridicule; he
remarks, " we may obferve, that in our own
" nation the moft fuccefsful criticifm or me-
" thod of refutation, is that which borders moft
" on the manner of the earlieft Greek comedy.
" The highly rated burlefque poem written on
" the fubject of our religious controverfies in
" the laft age, is a fufficient token of this kind;
" and that juftly admired piece of comic wit
" given us fome time after by an author of the
" higheft quality, has furnifhed our beft wits,
" in all their controverfies even in religion and
" politics, as well as in the affairs of wit and
" learning, with the moft effectual and enter-
" taining method of expofing folly, pedantry,
" falfe reafon and ill writing. And without
" fome fuch tolerated manner of criticifm as
" this, how grofsly we might have been impofed
" on, and fhould continue to be for the future,

* Lord Shaftefbury.

" by

" by many pieces of dogmatical rhetorick and
" pedantic wit, may eafily be apprehended by
" thofe who know any thing of the ftate of
" letters in our nation, or are in the leaft fitted
" to judge of the manner of the common poets,
" or formal authors of the times."

It had been finifhed before the end of 1664,
and had been feveral times rehearfed; the players
were perfect in their parts, and all things in
readinefs for acting, before the great plague in
1665, which then prevented it : but what was
then intended was very different from what now
appears. In that he called his poet Bilboa, by
which name Sir Robert Howard was the perfon
pointed at. But from that time till the year
1671, when it was firft acted, many plays came
forth writ in heroic rhyme ; and on the death of
Sir William d'Avenant in 1669, whom Mr.
Dryden fucceeded as laureat, thefe became ftill
in greater vogue from Mr. Dryden's example,
who was much admired and highly applauded,
though he fell into the wild and licentious humour of thofe times. The duke therefore refolved
to change the name of his poet from Bilboa to
Bayes, and through the whole play he miffes

no

no opportunity of expofing the hero and his works.

Mr. Dryden was fenfibly touched thereby, and in revenge for the ridicule thrown upon him in this piece, he expofed the duke under the name of Zimri, in his Abfalom and Achitophel, in the following beautiful lines :

A man fo various, that he feem'd to be
Not one, but all mankind's epitome.
Stiff in opinion, always in the wrong,
Was every thing by ftarts, and nothing long;
But in the courfe of one revolving moon,
Was chymift, fidler, ftatefman and buffoon :
Then all for women, painting, rhyming, drinking,
Befides ten thoufand freaks that died in thinking.
Bleft madman, who could every hour employ
With fomething new to wifh or to enjoy !
Railing and praifing were his ufual themes,
And both (to fhew his judgment) in extremes ;
So over violent, or over civil,
That every man with him was god or devil.
In fquandering wealth was his peculiar art ;
Nothing went unrewarded but defert.
Beggar'd by fools, whom ftill he found too late,
He had his jeft, but they had his eftate.
He laugh'd himfelf from court, then fought relief
By forming parties, but could ne'er be chief;

For

For spite of him, the weight of busness fell
On Absalom, and wise Achitophel.
Thus wicked but in will, of means bereft,
He left not faction, but of that was left.

Mr. Horace Walpole, with that justness which mark all his writings, observes, The portrait drawn by Dryden is admirable, but Bayes is an original creation. Dryden satirized Buckingham; Villiers in the Rehearsal made Dryden *satirise himself*. The same gentleman remarks it as an instance of astonishing quickness, that the Duke being present at one of the plays of Dryden, where a lover says,

My wound is great because it is so small,

his Grace cried out,

Then it would be greater were it none at all.

The play was instantly *damn'd*.

On the 7th of June, 1671, he was installed Chancellor of the University of Cambridge; and he entertained that learned body nobly at York-house, where his father had done on the same occasion forty years before: and during this year he advised the declaration of indulgence, published March 15, for suspending the penal laws against dissenters. In 1672 he

was

was fent a fecond time, together with the earls of Arlington and lord Hallifax, to the French king, then at Utrecht, to concert meafures fe-cretly for carrying on the fecond Dutch war. Upon the meeting of the parliament the enfuing year, a complaint being made of him in the houfe of commons, for revealing the king's councils, and correfponding with his enemies, in his defence of himfelf before that houfe he confeffed fome part of his bad adminiftration, and betrayed more of his affociate Arlington. In 1674, he again fell under the difpleafure of the king, and ceafing to be ufeful, Charles de-clared the chancellorfhip of the univerfity of Cambridge vacant, and the duke of Monmouth was chofen in his room. About this time he joined the nonconformifts, and the earl of Shaftefbury, in their oppofition to the court, againft the famous bill to prevent the danger that may arife from perfons difaffected to the govern-ment, which was brought into the houfe of lords in April 1675. In this bill was inferted the teft, by which, befides the oaths required of ma-giftrates in corporations, viz. I A. B. do de-clare that it is not lawful upon any pretence
what-

whatfoever to take up arms againft the king, there was added the following: *I A. B. do fwear, that I will not endeavour an alteration of the proteftant religion, eftablifhed by law in the church of England, nor will I endeavour any alteration in the government of the kingdom, in church or ftate, as it is by law eftablifhed.* This was propofed to be taken by all who enjoyed any beneficial offices, ecclefiaftical, civil or military, and by all privy counfellors, juftices of the peace, and both houfes of parliament. The court party efpoufed the bill with great zeal, and it was as ftrenuoufly oppofed by the country party, who looked on it *as a project to divide the proteftants, and to ftrengthen the popifh party.* The chief fpeakers for the bill were the lord treafurer Danby, the lord keeper Finch, and the bifhops Morley and Ward. Thofe on the fide of oppofition were the lords Hallifax and Holles, the earls of Salifbury and Shaftefbury, and the duke of Buckingham. Thefe, with the marquis of Winchefter, nine earls, and feven barons, entered their proteft againft it, " conceiving that any bills which " impofeth an oath on the peers with a penalty, " as doth that upon refufal of that oath, they

" fhall

" fhall be made incapable of fetting and voting
" in their houfe, as it is a thing unprecedented
" in former times, fo it is in their opinion the
" higheft invafion of the liberties and privileges
" of the peerage that poffibly may be, and moft
" deftructive of the freedom which they ought
" to enjoy as members of parliament; becaufe
" the privileges of fetting and voting in parlia-
" ment is an honour they have by birth, and a
" right fo inherent in them, as that nothing can
" take away, but what by the law of the land
" muft withal take away their lives, and cor-
" rupt their blood." And when the bill was
committed, they got in this provifo, *That it
fhould be no hindrance to their free fpeaking and
voting in parliament.* The bill mifcarried by the
king's proroguing the parliament. The duke's
oppofition was perfectly confiftent to his tole-
rating principles ; for the October following he
brought a bill into the houfe of lords for tole-
rating the diffenters, and was appointed one of
the managers in a conference between the two
houfes of parliament upon the point of the ju-
rifdiction of the upper houfe. The king, defirous to check the heats and animofities occafioned

VOL. I.   c   by

by the difputes, prorogued the parliament in
November till February 1677, which being up-
wards of a year, the duke of Buckingham made
a fpeech that day, to fhew that in this proroga-
tion his majefty had exceeded the bounds of his
prerogative, and attempted to prove from ancient
ftatutes the parliament was diffolved. He *ludi-
croufly* remarked, the ancient laws of the realm
are not like *women*, for they are not one jot the
worfe for being *old:* he perfifted in his affertion
that the king had exceeded his prerogative, and
that the parliament was diffolved. He was fe-
conded by the earls of Shaftefbury and Salifbury,
and lord Wharton; great debates arofe in the
houfe; a motion was made that the four lords
be committed to the tower, for contempt of the
authority and being of the prefent parliament,
there to remain during the pleafure of his majefty
and the houfe of peers. The duke, while lord
Anglefey was fpeaking againft the commitment,
left the houfe. The lords, in a rage at his
withdrawing himfelf, defigned to addrefs the
king for a proclamation againft him; the duke,
forefeeing the event, appeared next day in his
place; The court lords immediately cried out,

To

2

To the bar! His grace arofe, and turning their proceedings into a jeft, faid, " *He begged their* " *lordſhip's pardon for retiring the night before;* " *that they very well knew the exact œconomy he* " *kept in his family, and perceiving their lordſhips* " *intended he ſhould be ſome time or other in another* " *place, he only went home to ſet his houſe in order,* " *and was now come to ſubmit to their lordſhips* " *pleaſure,*" which was to ſend him to the Tower after the Earls of Shaftefbury and Salifbury, and the Lord Wharton *; but upon a petition to the king, he was difcharged from thence the May following. After this he continued in oppofition to the court, and exerted himfelf greatly againft

---

* The Earl of Shaftefbury being jealous of the Duke fetting himfelf up for the head of his party, ufed to fpeak flightingly of him, as a man *inconftant* and *giddy,* which the other hearing, refented. The Duke of Buckingham, the Earl of Salifbury and Lord Wharton being difcharged on their fubmiffion, and only the Earl of Shaftefbury continued in the Tower; the earl looked out of window as his grace was taking coach, and faid, " What, my lord, " are you going to leave us?" " Aye, my lord," replied the duke, " fuch *giddy-headed fellows as I can never ſtay* " *long in a place.*" The Earl of Shaftefbury was confined above a year.

all

all concerned in the popifh plot. In 1680 having fold Wallingford-Houfe, he purchafed a houfe at Dowgate, and refided there, joining with the Earl of Shaftefbury in attempting to get them-felves elected into the magiftracy of the City of London, and fpiriting up the citizens to a vi-gorous oppofition to adminiftration. In 1685 he publifhed a fhort difcourfe upon the reafon-ablenefs of men's having a religion or worfhip of God; this tract was immediately anfwered; on which the duke publifhed a ludicrous and excel-lent reply, which was alfo remarked on.

The duke now deeply felt the unlimited con-fidence he repofed in his city friends and fer-vants; his own extravagant tafte for magni-ficence, and thofe infatiable drainers, chymiftry, mufic, and building in that fort of architecture which Cicero calls *infanæ fubftructiones*, and which the duke ufually denominated his folly, had impoverifhed his fortune. His irregular and unftable conduct in his political capacity having ruined him with parties, his creditors growing clamorous, and his health being greatly impaired, at the death of Charles II. he retired to his own manor of Helmfley, in Yorkfhire. King Charles
loved

loved his company, and well knowing his character, pardoned his follies. The duke had formerly affected to fear an affaffination from James,
with whom he had had too many differences to
think his prefence acceptable at court. The
zeal of the king on hearing of his grace's ficknefs, was defirous of converting him to the church
of Rome, and accordingly fent Father Fitz-
gerald to him; the prieft's arguments were foiled
by the Duke's inimitable turn of wit.

During his retirement he paffed his time in
hunting and entertaining his friends, which he
did a fortnight before his death with great plea-
fantry and hofpitality.

Returning from a fox-hunt, he fat on the
damp ground, which threw him into an ague
and fever; he retired to a tenant's houfe at
Kirby Moor Side, a lordfhip of his own near
Helmfley; diffatisfied with his miferable fitua-
tion, he fent to his old fervant, Mr. Brian Fairfax, to defire him to provide him a bed at his
houfe, at Bifhop-Hill, in York; the next morning another meffenger acquainted Mr. Fairfax
his grace's life was defpaired of. Fairfax fet out
poft; when he arrived he found the duke, accom-
panied

panied by the Earl of Arran, fon to Duke Hamilton, who hearing of his ficknefs, vifited him in his way to Scotland. The duke looked earneftly at Fairfax, but was unable to fpeak. Mr. Fairfax enquired of a gentleman of integrity who was prefent, what had been faid or done before his grace became fpeechlefs, who told him fome queftions had been afked him about his eftate, to which he gave no anfwer; that on enquiring if he chofe to have the minifter of the parifh fent for, he was alfo filent; but on afking whether he chofe a prieft to wait on him, he anfwered with great vehemence, No, no! The violence of the fever feems from the firft to have deprived him of his faculties, neverthelefs a minifter was fent for, who adminiftered the facrament to him.

On the 16th of April, 1688, the third day of his illnefs, he expired quietly on his bed, aged fixty, the fate of few of his predeceffors in the title of Buckingham. His body was embalmed and brought to Weftminfter Abbey, and there depofited in the vault with his father and brother's, in Henry VIIth's chapel.

Thus died in contempt and mifery, circumftances moft unworthy of himfelf, the great Duke

of

of Buckingham *; a melancholy example of the proftitution of talents. In his perfon he was tall, active, and of a noble prefence, irrefiftable in his converfation, poffeffed of great livelinefs of wit, and a peculiar faculty of turning all things into ridicule, with bold figures and natural defcriptions; though few owed more to fortune, none ever made a worfe ufe of her favours; with an

* His end is pathetically defcribed by Mr. Pope in his epiftle to Lord Bathurft, in the following verfes.

In the worft inn's worft room, with matt half-hung,
The floors of plaifter, and the walls of dung:
On once a flock-bed, but repair'd with ftraw,
With tape-ty'd curtains never meant to draw,
The George and Garter dangling from that bed
Where tawdry yellow ftrove with dirty red,
Great Villjers lies—Alas! how chang'd from him,
That life of pleafure, and that foul of whim!
Gallant and gay, in Cliveden's proud alcove,
The bow'r of wanton Shrewfbury and Love;
Or juft as gay, at council, in a ring
Of mimick ftatefmen, and their merry king.
No wit to flatter, left of all his ftore;
No fool to laugh at, which he valued more.
There, victor of his health, of fortune, friends,
And fame, this lord of ufelefs thoufands ends.

ample

ample eſtate, yet always in diſtreſs; a ſpend-
thrift without magnificence; extravagant without the leaſt ſymptom of generoſity. He was
vain, but not proud; eager for reputation, but
careleſs of his honour; ſuperſtitious in his diſpoſition, without religion. Pleaſure, frolick, or
extravagant diverſion was his only delight. It
is much to be lamented, that a man of ſuch un-
common talents ſhould be ſubject to unaccount-
able weakneſſes, and devoid of virtue.

T. E.

THE

THE

REHEARSAL;

WITH NOTES.

CONTAINING

A CRITICAL VIEW OF THE AUTHORS,

AND

THEIR WRITINGS,

THAT ARE EXPOSED IN THAT CELEBRATED PLAY.

WRITTEN BY HIS GRACE

GEORGE VILLIERS, LATE DUKE OF BUCKINGHAM.

PLAYS MENTIONED IN THE NOTES TO THE REHEARSAL.

I. THE Loſt Lady; by Sir William Barcley.

II. Love and Honour; by Sir William D'Avenant.

III. Love and Friendſhip;

IV. Pandora;

} by Sir William Killigrew.

V. Siege of Rhodes, part I. by Sir William D'Avenant.

VI. Play-houſe to be lett; by colonel Henry Howard.

VII. United Kingdoms.

VIII. Slighted Maid; by Sir Robert Stapleton.

IX. Wild Gallant; by Mr. Dryden.

X. Engliſh Monſieur; by Mr. James Howard.

XI. The Villain; by major Tho. Porter.

XII. The

XII. The Prologue to the Maiden Queen; by Mr. Dryden.

XIII. The Amorous Prince; by Mrs. Behn.

XIV. Tyrannic Love and Prologue; by Mr. Dryden.

XV. Granada, 2 parts, by Mr. Dryden.

XVI. Matriage A-la-mode; by Mr. Dryden.

XVII. Love in a Nunnery; by Mr. Dryden.

P R O L O G U E.

WE might well call this short mock-play of ours
A poesy made of weeds, instead of flowers;
Yet such have been presented to your noses,
And there are such, I fear, who thought 'em roses.
Would some of 'em were here, to see this night,
What stuff it is in which they took delight.
Here, brisk, insipid rogues, for wit, let fall   X
Sometimes dull sense; but oftener none at all:
There, strutting heroes, with a grim-fac'd train,
Shall brave the gods, in king Cambyses vein:
For (changeing rules, of late, as if men writ
In spite of reason, nature, art and wit)
Our poets make us laugh at tragedy,
And with their comedies they make us cry.
Now, criticks, do your worst, that here are met;
For, like a rock, I have hedg'd in my bet.
If you approve; I shall assume the state
Of those high-flyers whom I imitate:
And justly too, for I will teach you more
Than ever they would let you know before:
I will not only shew the feats they do,
But give you all their reasons for 'em too.
Some honour may to me from hence arise: ⎫
But if, by my endeavours, you grow wise,   ⎬
And what you once so prais'd, shall now despise; ⎭
Then I'll cry out, swell'd with poetic rage,
'Tis I, John Lacy, have reform'd your stage.

THE ACTORS NAMES.

Bayes,
Johnson,
Smith,
2 Kings of Brentford,
Prince Prettymen,
Prince Volscius,
Gentleman Usher,
Physician,
Drawcansir,
General,
Lieutenant-general,
Cordelio,

Tom Thimble,
Fisherman,
Shirley,
Sun,
Thunder,
Players,
Soldiers,
Two heralds,
Four cardinals,
Judges, Mayor, Mutes.
Serjeants at
   arms.

W O M E N.

Amaryllis,
Cloris,
Parthenope,
Pallas,

Lightning,
Moon,
Earth,

Attendants of Men and Women.

Scene B R E N T F O R D.

THE

REHEARSAL.

ACT I.   SCENE I.

Johnſon and Smith.

Johnſ. **H**ONEST Frank! I am glad to ſee thee with all my heart. How long haſt thou been in town?

Smi. Faith not above an hour: and, if I had not met you here, I had gone to look you out; for I long to talk with you freely, of all the ſtrange new things we have heard in the country.

Johnſ. And by my troth, I have long'd as much to laugh with you, at all the impertinent, dull, fantaſtical things, we are tir'd out with here.

Smi. Dull and fantaſtick! that's an excellent compoſition. Pray what are our men of buſineſs doing?

Johnſ. I ne'er enquire after 'em. Thou knoweſt my humour lies another way. I love to pleaſe myſelf as much, and to trouble others as little as I can: and therefore do naturally avoid the company of thoſe ſolemn fops; who, being incapable of reaſon, and inſenſible of wit and pleaſure, are

B 4   always

always looking grave, and troubling one another, in hopes to be thought men of bufinefs.

Smi. Indeed, I have ever obferv'd, that your grave lookers are the dulleft of men.

Johnf. Ay, and of birds, and beafts too : your graveft bird is an owl, and your graveft beaft is an afs.

Smi. Well, but how doft thou pafs thy time ?

Johnf. Why, as I ufe to do; eat, and drink as well as I can, have a fhe-friend to be private with in the afternoon, and fometimes fee a play : Where are fuch things (*Frank*) fuch hideous, monftrous things, that it has almoft made me forfwear the ftage, and refolve to apply myfelf to the folid nonfenfe of your men of bufinefs, as the more in-genious paftime.

Smi. I have heard indeed, you have had lately many new plays ; and our country wits commend 'em.

Johnf. Ay, fo do fome of our city wits too ; but they are of the new kind of wits.

Smi. New kind ! what kind is that ?

Johnf. Why, your virtuofi, your civil perfons, your drolls : fellows that fcorn to imitate nature ; but are given altogether to elevate and furprize.

Smi.

Smi. Elevate and furprife! pr'ythee make me underftand the meaning of that.

Johnf. Nay, by my troth; that's a hard matter: I don't underftand that myfelf. 'Tis a phrafe they have got among them, to exprefs their no-meaning by. I'll tell you, as near as I can, what it is. Let me fee: 'tis fighting, loving, fleeping, rhiming, dying, dancing, finging, crying: and every thing, but thinking and fenfe.

Mr. Bayes *paffes over the ftage.*

Bayes. Your moft obfequious, and moft obfervant, very fervant, Sir.

Johnf. So, this is an author! I'll go fetch him to you.

Smi. No pr'ythee let him alone.

Johnf. Nay, by the lord I'll have him.

[*Goes after him.*

Here he is, I have caught him. Pray Sir, now for my fake, will you do a favour to this friend of mine?

Bayes. Sir, it is not within my fmall capacity to do favours, but receive 'em; efpecially from a perfon that does wear the honourable title you are

pleas'd

pleas'd to impofe, Sir, upon this-------Sweet Sir, your fervant.

Smi. Your humble fervant, Sir.

Johnf. But wilt thou do me a favour now?

Bayes. Ay, Sir: What is't?

Johnf. Why, to tell him the meaning of thy laft play.

Bayes. How, Sir, the meaning? do you mean the plot?

Johnf. Ay, ay; any thing.

Bayes. Faith Sir, the intrigo's now quite out of my head; but I have a new one, in my pocket, that I may fay is a virgin; it has never yet been blown upon. I muft tell you one thing, 'tis all new wit; and though I fay it, a better than my laft: and you know well enough how that took. * In fine, it fhall read, and write, and act, and plot, and fhew, ay, and pit, box, and gallery it, with any play in Europe. This morning is it's

---

* *In fine, it fhall read, and write, and act, and plot, and fhew, ay, and pit, box, and gallery it, with any play in Europe.* " This was the ufual language of the honoura-
" ble Edward Howard Efq; at the rehearfal of his
plays."

laft

laſt rehearſal in their habits, and all that, as it is
to be acted; and if you, and your friend will do it
but the honour to ſee it in its virgin attire, tho'
perhaps it may bluſh, I ſhall not be aſham'd to
diſcover it unto you ┤-----I think it is in this
pocket.

[*Puts his hand in his pocket.*

Johnſ. Sir, I confeſs, I am not able to anſwer
you in this new way; but if you pleaſe to lead, I
ſhall be glad to follow you; and I hope my friend
will do ſo too.

Smi. Sir, I have no buſineſs ſo conſiderable, as
ſhould keep me from your company.

Bayes. Yes, here it is. No, cry you mercy: this
is my book of Drama Common-places; the mother
of many other plays.

Johnſ. Drama Common-places! Pray what's
that?

Bayes. Why, Sir, ſome certain helps, that we
men of art have found it convenient to make
uſe of.

Smi. How, Sir, helps for wit?

Bayes. Ay, Sir, that's my poſition. And I do
here aver, that no man yet the ſun e'er ſhone
upon

upon has parts sufficient to furnish out a stage, except it were by the help of these my rules.*

Johns. What are those rules, I pray?

Bayes. Why Sir, my first rule is the rule of transversion, or *regula duplex:* changing verse into prose, or prose into verse, *alternative* as you please.

Smi. Well, but how is this done by rule, Sir?

Bayes. Why, thus, Sir; nothing so easy when understood; I take a book in my hand, either at home or elsewhere, for that's all one, if there be any wit in't, as there is no book but has some, I transverse it; that is, if it be prose, put it into verse, (but that takes up some time) and if it be verse, put it into prose.

Johns. Methinks, Mr. Bayes, that putting verse into prose should be calling transposing.

* *These my rules.*

He who wrote this, not without pain and thought
From French and English theatres, has brought
Th' exactest rules by which a play is wrought,

The unity of action, place and time;
The scenes unbroken; and a mingled chime
Of Johnson's humour, with Corneille's rhime.

Prologue to the Maiden Queen.
Bayes.

Bayes. By my troth, Sir, 'tis a very good notion, and hereafter it shall be so.

Smi. Well, Sir, and what d'ye do with it then?

Bayes. Make it my own. 'Tis so chang'd that no man can know it. My next rule is the rule of record by way of table-book. Pray observe.

Johnſ. We hear you, Sir: go on.

Bayes. As thus, I come into a coffee-houſe, or ſome other place where witty men reſort; I make as if I minded nothing: (do you mark?) but as ſoon as any one ſpeaks, pop I ſlap it down, and make that too my own.

Johnſ. But, Mr. Bayes, are you not ſometimes in danger of their making you reſtore, by force, what you have gotten thus, by art?

Bayes. No, Sir; the world's unmindful: they never take notice of theſe things.

Smi. But pray, Mr. Bayes, amongſt all your other rules, have you no one rule for Invention?

Bayes. Yes, Sir, that's my third rule that I have here in my pocket.

Smi. What rule can that be I wonder!

Bayes. Why. Sir, when I have any thing to invent, I never trouble my head about it, as other men do; but preſently turn over this book,

2 and

and there I have, at one view, all that Perſius, Montaigne, Seneca's Tragedies, Horace, Juvenal, Claudian, Pliny, Plutarch's Lives, and the reſt, have ever thought upon this ſubject; and ſo in a thrice, by leaving out a few words, or putting in others of my own, the buſineſs is done.

Johnſ. Indeed Mr. Bayes, this is as ſure, and compendious a way of wit as ever I heard of.

Bayes. Sirs, if you make the leaſt ſcruple of the efficacy of theſe my rules, do but come to the play-houſe, and you ſhall judge of 'em by the effects.

Smi. We'll follow you, Sir.   [*Exeunt.*

Enter three Players upon the Stage.

1 *Play.* Have you your part perfect?

2 *Play.* Yes I have it without book; but I don't underſtand how it is to be ſpoken.

3 *Play.* And mine is ſuch a one, as I can't gueſs for my life what humour I'm to be in; whether angry, melancholy, merry, or in love. I don't know what to make on't.

1 *Play.* Phoo! the author will be here preſently and he'll tell us all. You muſt know, this is the new way of writing, and theſe hard things pleaſe forty times better than the old plain way.

For,

For, look you, Sir, the grand defign upon the ftage is to keep the auditors in fufpence; for to guefs prefently at the plot, and the fenfe tires them before the end of the firft act: now, here every line furprifes you, and brings in matter. And then, for fcenes, cloaths and dances, we put quite down all that ever went before us; and thofe are the things, you know, that are effential to a play.

2 Play. Well, I am not of thy mind; but, fo it gets us money, 'tis no great matter.

Enter Bayes, Johnfon *and* Smith.

Bayes. Come, come in, gentlemen. Y'are very welcome Mr.—a—Ha' you your part ready?

1 Play. Yes, Sir.

Bayes. But do you underftand the true humour of it.

1 Play. Ay, Sir, pretty well.

Bayes. And Amaryllis, how does fhe do? Does not her armour become her?

3 Play. O, admirably!

Bayes. I'll tell you now a pretty conceit. What do you think I'll make 'em call her anon, in this play.

Smi. What, I pray?

Bayes

Bayes, Why, I make 'em call her Amaryllis, becaufe of her amour.   Ha, ha, ha.

Johnf. That will be very well indeed.

Bayes. Ay, it's a pretty little rogue; I knew her face would fet off armour extremely; and to tell you true, I writ that part only for her.   You muft know fhe is my miftrefs *.

Johnf. Then I know another thing, little Bayes, that thou haft had her.

Bayes. No, not yet; but I am fure I fhall: For I have talk'd bawdy to her already.

Johnf. Haft thou, faith? Pr'ythee how was that?

Bayes. Why, Sir, there is in the French tongue, a certain criticifm, which, by the variation of the mafculine adjective inftead of the feminine, makes a quite different fignification of the word: as for example, *Ma vie,* is my life; but, if before *vie* you put *mon* inftead of *ma,* you make it bawdy.

Johnf. Very true.

Bayes. Now, Sir, I, having obferv'd this, fet a

* *I writ that part only for her. You muft know fhe is my miftrefs.*] " The part of Amaryllis was acted by Mrs.
" Anne Reeves, who, at that time, was kept by Mr. Bayes.

trap

trap for her, the other day in the tiring-room; for this, faid I, *Adieu bel efperanfa de ma vie*; (which I'gad is very pretty:) to which fhe anfwered, I vow, almoft as prettily every jot; for, faid fhe, *Songez a ma vie, monfieur*; whereupon I prefently fnapp'd this upon her; *Non, non, Madam*-----*Songez vous à mon*, by gad, and nam'd the thing directly to her.

Smi. This is one of the richeft ftories, Mr. Bayes, that ever I heard of.

Bayes. Ay, let me alone, I'gad, when I get to 'em; I'll nick 'em, I warrant you: but I'm a little nice; for you muft know, at this time, I am kept by another woman in this city.

Smi. How kept? for what?·

Bayes. Why, for a Beau Garçon: I am i'fackins.

Smi. Nay, then we fhall never have done.

Bayes. And the rogue is fo fond of me, Mr. Johnfon, that, I vow to God, I know not what to do with myfelf.

Johnf. Do with thyfelf! no; I wonder how thou canft make a fhift to hold out at this rate.

Bayes. O devil, I can toil like a horfe; only fometimes it makes me melancholy; and then I

VOL. I. C vow

vow to gad, for a whole day together, I am not able
to fay you one good thing if it were to fave my life.

Smi. That we do verily believe, Mr. Bayes.

Bayes. And that's the only thing, I'gad, which
mads me in my amours; for I'll tell you, as a
friend, Mr. Johnfon, my acquaintance, I hear,
begin to give out that I am dull: now I am the
fartheft from it in the whole world, I'gad, but
only forfooth, they think I am fo, becaufe I can
fay nothing.

Johnf. Phoo, pox. That's ill-natur'dly done
of 'em.

Bayes. Ay, gad, there's no trufting o' thefe
rogues; but--a--Come, let's fit down. Look you
Sirs, the chief hinge of this play, upon which the
whole plot moves and turns, and that caufes the
variety of all the feveral accidents, which, you
know, are the thing in nature that makes up the
grand refinement of a play, is that I fuppofe * two

* *I fuppofe two kings of the fame place: as for example,*
at Brentford; for I love to write familiarly. " Colonel
" Henry Howard, fon of Thomas earl of Berkfhire, made
" a play, called The united Kingdoms, which had two
" kings in it. This, it is generally believed, gave our
" noble author juft occafion to fet up two kings at Brent-
" ford; though others are of opinion, his grace had the two
royal

kings of the fame place: as for example, at Brentford; for I love to write familiarly. Now, the
people having the fame relations to 'em both; the
fame affections, the fame duty, the fame obedience, and all that; are divided amongft themfelves
in point of devoir and intereft, how to behave
themfelves equally between 'em : thefe kings differ-
ing fometimes in particulars; tho', in the main,
they agree. (I know not whether I make myfelf
well underftood.)

Johnf. I did not obferve you, Sir; pray, fay
that again.

Bayes. Why, look you, Sir, (nay I befeech you
be a little curious in taking notice of this, or elfe
you'll never underftand my notion of the thing)
the people being embarrafs'd by their equal ties
to both, and the fovereigns concern'd in a reci-

" royal brothers in his thoughts. The United kingdoms
" was acted at the Cock-pit in Drury-lane, foon after the
" Reftoration; but mifcarrying on the ftage, the author had
" the modefty not to print it, and therefore the reader cannot
" reafonably expect any particular paffages of it. Others
" are of opinion, that the two kings are meant in ridicule
" of Boabdelin and Abdalla, the two contending kings of
" Granada; and Mr. Dryden has, in moft of his ferious
" plays, two contending kings of the fame place.

procal

procal regard, as well to their own intereſt, as the good of the people; may make a certain kind of a-------you underſtand me-------upon which, there does ariſe ſeveral diſputes, turmoils, heart-burnings, and all that----In fine, you'll apprehend it better when you ſee it.   [*Exit to call the Players.*

Smi. I find the author will be very much obliged to the players, if they can make any ſenſe out of this.

Enter Bayes.

Bayes. Now, gentlemen, I would fain aſk your opinion of one thing. I have made a prologue and an epilogue, which may both ſerve for either; (that is, the prologue for the epilogue, or the epilogue for the prologue) [do you mark?] nay, they may both ſerve too, I'gad for any other play as well as this.

Smi. Very well.   That's indeed artificial. *is continued*

Bayes. And I would fain aſk your judgments, now, which of them would do beſt for the prologue? for, you muſt know, there is in nature but two ways of making very good prologues.   The one is by civility, by inſinuation, good language, and all that---a---in a manner, ſteal your plaudit

from

from the courtefy of the auditors : the other, by making ufe of fome certain perfonal things, which may keep a hank upon fuch cenfuring perfons, as cannot otherways, I'gad, in nature, be hindred from being too free with their tongues. To which end, my firft prologue is,* that I come out in a long black veil, and a great huge hangman be-hind me, with a furr'd cap, and his fword drawn; and there tell 'em plainly, that if, out of good nature, they will not like my play, I'gad, I'll e'en kneel down, and he fhall cut my head off. Where-upon they all fall a clapping---a---

Smi. Ay, but fuppofe they don't.

Bayes. Suppofe! Sir, you may fuppofe what you pleafe, I have nothing to do with your fup-pofe, Sir; nor am not at all mortified at it : not at all, Sir; I'gad, not one jot, Sir. Suppofe, quotha!----ha, ha, ha. [*Walks away.*

Johnf. Phoo! pr'ythee, Bayes, don't mind what he fays: he is a fellow newly come out of the country, he knows nothing of what's the re-lifh here of the town.

Bayes. If I writ, Sir, to pleafe the country, I

* *To which end, my firft prologue is,* &c.] " Vide the
" two prologues to the Maiden Queen.

fhould

ſhould have follow'd the old plain way: but I write for ſome perſons of quality, and peculiar friends of mine, that underſtand what fiame and power in writing is; and they do me right, Sir, to approve of what I do.

Johnſ. Ay, ay, they will clap, I warrant you; never fear it.

Bayes. I'm ſure the deſign's good; that cannot be deny'd. And then, for language, I'gad, I defy 'em all, in nature, to mend it. * Beſides, Sir, I have printed above a hundred ſheets of paper, to inſinuate the plot into the boxes; and withal, have appointed two or three dozen of my friends to be ready in the pit, who I'm ſure will clap, and ſo the reſt you know muſt follow; and then, pray, Sir, what becomes of your ſuppoſe? ha, ha, ha.

Johnſ. Nay, if the buſineſs be ſo well laid, it cannot miſs.

Bayes. I think ſo, Sir; and therefore would

* *Beſides, I have printed above a hundred ſheets of paper, to inſinuate the plot into the boxes.*] There were printed papers given the audience before the acting of the Indian Emperor, telling them that it was the ſequel of the Indian Queen, part of which play was written by Mr. Bayes.

chuſe

chufe this to be the prologue. For, if I could engage 'em to clap, before they fee the play, you
know it would be fo much the better, becaufe they
were engaged; for let a man write never fo well,
there are, now a-days, a fort of perfons they call
criticks, that I'gad*, have no more wit in them
than fo many hobby-horfes; but they'll laugh at
you, Sir, and find fault, and cenfure things, that,
I'gad, I'm fure they are not able to do themfelves.
A fort of envious perfons, that emulate the glo-
ries of perfons of parts, and think to build their
fame, by calumniation of perfons, that, I'gad,
to my knowledge, of all perfons in the world
are, in nature, the perfons that do as much defpife all that as---a---In fine, I'll fay no more of
'em.

* *I'gad, I vow to gad.*] And all that, is the conftant
ftile of Failer in the Wild Gallant; for which take this
fpecimen.
  " *Failer.* Really, madam, I look upon you as a perfon
" of fuch worth, and all that, that, I vow to gad I honour
" you of all perfons in the world; and, tho' I am a perfon
" that am inconfiderable, in the world, and all that, ma-
" dam, yet, for a perfon of your worth and excellency,
" I would, &c.

Johnf. Nay, you have faid enough of 'em, in all confcience ; I'm fure more than they'll e'er be able to anfwer.

Bayes. Why, I'll tell you, Sir, fincerely, and *bona fide* ; were it not for the fake of fome ingenious perfons, and choice female fpirits, that have a value for me, I would fee 'em all hang'd, I'gad, fee 'em all hang'd before I would e'er fet pen to paper, but let them live in ignorance like ingrates.

Johnf. Ay, marry! that were a way to be reveng'd of 'em indeed ; and, if I were in your place now, I would do fo.

Bayes. No, Sir; there are certain ties * upon me, that I cannot be difengaged from ; otherways I would. But pray, Sir, how do you like my hangman ?

Smi. By my troth, Sir, I fhould like him very well. '

Bayes. But how do you like it, Sir ? (for I fee you can judge) would you have it for a prologue, or an epilogue.

---

* *Bayes. No, Sir, there are certain ties upon me, that I cannot be difengag'd from.*] Mr. Dryden had contracted with the king's company of actors in the year 1668, for a whole Share, to write them four plays a-year.

Johnf.

Johnf. Faith, Sir, 'tis fo good, let it e'en ferve for both.

Bayes. No, no; that won't do. Befides, I have made another.

Johnf. What other, Sir?

Bayes. Why, Sir, my other is thunder and lightning.

Johnf. That's greater, I'd rather ftick to that.

Bayes. Do you think fo? I'll tell you then; tho' there have been many witty prologues written of late, yet, I think, you'll fay this is a *non pareillo*: I'm fure no body has hit upon it yet. For here, Sir, I make my prologue to be a dialogue; and as in my firft, you fee I ftrive to oblige the auditors by civility, by good nature, good language, and all that; fo, in this, by the other way, *in terrorem*, I chufe for the perfons, Thunder and Lightning. Do you apprehend the conceit?

Johnf. Phoo, pox! then you have it cock-fure. They'll be hang'd before they'll dare affront an author, that has 'em at that lock.

Bayes. I have made, too, one of the moft delicate, dainty fimiles in the whole world, I'gad, if I knew how to apply it.

Smi. Let's hear it, I pray you.

Bayes.

Bayes. 'Tis an Allufion of love.

* So boar and fow, when any ftorm is nigh,
Snuff up, and fmell it gathering in the fky:
Boar beckons fow to trot in chefnut groves,
And there confummate their unfinifh'd loves;
Penfive in mud they wallow all alone,
And fnore, and gruntle to each others moan.

How do you like it now, ha?

Johnf. Faith, 'tis extraordinary fine; and very
applicable to thunder and lightning, methinks,
becaufe it fpeaks of a ftorm.

Bayes. I'gad, and fo it does, now I think on't;
Mr. Johnfon, I thank you; and I put it in *profecto.*
Come out Thunder and Lightning.

* *So boar and fow, &c.*] Thefe verfes are in rid cule
of the following lines in the conqueft of Granada, part II.
page 48.
  " So two kind turtles, when a ftorm is nigh,
  " Look up, and fee it gath'ring in the fky:
  " Each calls his mate to fhelter in the groves,
  " Leaving in murmurs their unfinifh'd loves;
  " Perch'd on fome dropping branch, they fit alone,
  " And coo, and hearken to each others moan.

Enter

Enter Thunder *and* Lightning.

Thun. I am the bold thunder.

Bayes. Mr. Cartwright, pr'ythee ſpeak that a little louder, and with a hoarſe voice. I am the bold thunder! Pſhaw! Speak it in a voice that thunders out indeed: I am the bold Thunder.

Thun. I am the bold thunder.*

Light. The briſk lightning I.

Bayes. Nay, but you muſt be quick and nimble. The briſk lightning I. That's my meaning.

Thun. I am the braveſt Heĉtor of the ſky.

Light. And I fair Helen, that made Heĉtor die.

Thun. I ſtrike men down.

Light. I fire the town.

Thun. Let criticks take heed how they grumble,
　　　　For then I begin for to rumble.

Light. Let the ladies allow us their graces,†
　　　　Or I'll blaſt all the paint on their faces,
　　　　And dry up their petre to foot.

---

* *I am the bold thunder.*] In ridicule of this paſſage,
　　" I am the evening dark as night.
　　　　　　　　　　　　　　Slighted Maid, p. 48.

† *Let the ladies allow us,* &c.]
　　" Let the men 'ware the ditches,
　　" Maids look to their breeches;
　　" We'll ſcratch them with briars and thorns.
　　　　　　　　　　　　　　Slighted Maid, p. 49.

Thun. Let the criticks look to't.

Light. Let the ladies look to't.

Thun. For thunder will do't.

Light. For lightning will ſhoot.

Thun. I'll give you daſh for daſh.

Light. I'll give you flaſh for flaſh.

Gallants I'll ſinge your feather.

Thun. I'll thunder you together.

Both. Look to't, look to't, we'll do't, we'll do't:
Look to't, we'll do't.   [*Twice or thrice repeated.*

Bayes. There's no more. 'Tis but a flaſh of a
prologue. A droll.   [*Exeunt ambo.*

Smi. Yes, 'tis ſhort indeed; but very terrible.

Bayes. Ay, when the ſimile's in it will do to a
miracle, I'gad. Come, come, begin the play.

Enter 1ſt Player.

1 *Play.* Sir, * Mr. Ivory is not come yet; but
he'll be here preſently, he's but two doors off.

---

* *Mr. Abraham Ivory, &c.*] Mr. Abraham Ivory had
formerly been a conſiderable actor of women's parts; but
afterwards ſtupify'd himſelf ſo far, with drinking ſtrong
waters, that, before the firſt acting of this farce, he was
fit for nothing, but to go of errands; for which, and
meer charity, the company allow'd him a weekly ſalary.

Bayes.

Bayes. Come then, gentlemen, let's go out and take a pipe of tobacco.   [*Exeunt.*

END OF THE FIRST ACT.

ACT II.   SCENE I.

Bayes, Johnſon, *and* Smith.

Bayes. NOW, Sir, becauſe I'll do nothing here that ever was done before, inſtead of beginning with a ſcene that diſcovers ſomething of the plot, I begin this play with a whiſper.*

Smi. Umph ! very new, indeed.

Bayes. Come, take your ſeats. Begin, Sirs.

Enter Gentleman-Uſher *and* Phyſician.

Phyſ. Sir, by your habit, I gueſs you to be the Gentleman-uſher of this ſumptuous place.

---

* *I begin this play with a whiſper.*] See the amorous prince, page 20, 22, 39, 69, where you will find, all the chief commands and directions are given in whiſpers.

" *Drake Sen.* Draw up our men ;

" and in low whiſpers give our orders out.

                              Play-houſe to be lett, p. 100.
                                             Uſh.

Ush. And by your gait and fashion, I should almost suspect, you rule the healths of both our noble kings, under the notion of physician.

Phys. You hit my function right.

Ush. And, you mine.

Phys. Then let's embrace.

Ush. Come.

Phys. Come.

Johns. Pray, Sir, who are those so very civil persons ?

Bayes. Why, Sir, the gentleman-usher, and physician of the two kings of Brentford.

Johns. But, pray then, how comes it to pass, that they know one another no better ?

Bayes. Phoo ! that's for the better carrying on of the plot.

Johns. Very well.

Phys. Sir, to conclude.

Smi. What, before he begins ?

Bayes. No, Sir, you must know, they had been a talking of this a pretty while without.

Smi. Where ? in the tiring-room ?

Bayes. Why, ay Sir. He's so dull ! Come speak again.

Phys. Sir, to conclude, the place you fill, has

more

more than amply exacted the talents of a wary pilot, and all thefe threatning ftorms, which, like impregnate clouds, hover o'er our heads, will, when they once are grafp'd but by the eye of reafon, melt into fruitful fhowers of bleffings on the people.

Bayes. Pray, mark that allegory. Is not that good ?

Johnf. Yes, that grafping of a ftorm, with the eye, is admirable.

Phyf. But yet fome rumours great are ftirring; and if Lorenzo fhould prove falfe, (which none but the gods can tell) you then perhaps would find that------ [*Whifpers.*

Bayes. Now he whifpers.

Ufh. Alone, do you fay ?

Phyf. No, attended with the noble---[*Whifpers.*

Bayes. Again.

Ufh. Who, he in gray ?

Phyf. Yes, and at the head of------[*Whifpers.*

Bayes. Pray, mark.

Ufh. Then, Sir, moft certain, 'twill in time appear.

Thefe are the reafons that have mov'd him to't.

Firft, he------ [*Whifpers.*

I *Bayes.*

Bayes. Now the other whifpers.

Ufh. Secondly, they------   [*Whifpers.*

Bayes. At it ftill.

Ufh. Thirdly, and laftly, both he, and they---
                              [*Whifpers.*

Bayes. Now they both whifper.

                    [*Exeunt Whifpering.*
Now gentlemen, pray tell me true, and without
flattery, is not this a very odd beginning of a
play?

Johnf. In troth, I think it is, Sir.   But why
two kings of the fame place?

Bayes. Why? Becaufe it's new; and that's it
I aim at.   I defpife your Johnfon and Beaumont,
that borrow'd all they writ from nature; I am for
fetching it purely out of my own fancy, I. ·

Smi. But what think you of Sir John Suckling?

Bayes. By gad, I am a better poet than he.

Smi. Well, Sir, but pray why all this whif-
pering.

Bayes. Why, Sir, (befides that it is new, as I
told you before) becaufe they are fuppofed to be
politicians; and matters of ftate ought not to be
divulg'd.

Smi. But then, Sir, why------

                 2   *Bayes.*

Bayes. Sir, if you'll but refpite your curiofity till the end of the fifth act, you'll find it a piece of patience not ill recompens'd. [*Goes to the door.*

Johnf. How doft thou like this Frank ? Is it not juft as I told thee ?

Smi. Why, I did never before this fee any thing in nature, and all that, (as Mr. Bayes fays) fo foolifh, but I could give fome guefs at what mov'd the fop to do it ; but this, I confefs, does go beyond my reach.

Johnf. It is all alike ; * Mr. Winterfhall has inform'd me of this play already. And I'll tell thee, Frank, thou fhalt not fee one fcene here worth one farthing, or like any thing thou canft imagine has ever been the practice of the world. And then, when he comes to what he calls good language, it is, as I told thee, very fantaftical, moft abominably dull, and not one word to the purpofe.

Smi. It does furprize me, I'm fure very much.

Johnf. Ay, but it won't do fo long : by that time thou haft feen a play or two, that I'll fhew

* *Mr. William Winterfhall,* &c.] Mr. Winterfhall was a moft excellent, judicious actor ; and the beft inftructor of others : he died in July, 1679.

thee,

thee, thou wilt be pretty well acquainted with this new kind of foppery.

Smi. Pox on't, but there's no pleafure in him; he's too grofs a fool to be laugh'd at.

Enter Bayes.

Johnf. I'll fwear, Mr. Bayes, you have done this fcene moft admirably; tho', I muft tell you, Sir, it is a very difficult matter to pen a whifper well.

Bayes. Ay, gentlemen, when you come to write yourfelves, o'my word, you'll find it fo.

Johnf. Have a care of what you fay, Mr. Bayes, for Mr. Smith there, I affure you, has written a great many fine things already.

Bayes. Has he, ifackins ? Why then pray, Sir, how do you do, when you write ?

Smi. Faith, Sir, for the moft part, I am in pretty good health.

Bayes. Ay, but I mean, what do you, when you write ?

Smi. I take pen, ink and paper, and fit down.

Bayes. Now, I write ftanding; that's one thing: and then another thing is, with what do you pre-pare yourfelf ?

Smi.

Smi. Prepare myfelf! what the devil does the fool mean?

Bayes. Why, I'll tell you now, what I do. * If I am to write familiar things, as fonnets to Armida, and the like, I make ufe of ftew'd prunes only; but when I have a grand defign in hand, I ever take phyfick, and let blood: for, when you would have pure fwiftnefs of thought, and fiery flights of fancy, you muft have a care of the penfive part. In fine, you muft purge the belly.

Smi. By my troth, Sir, this is a moft admirable receipt, for writing.

Bayes. Ay, 'tis my fecret; and in good earneft, I think one of the beft I have.

Smi. In good faith, Sir, and that may very well be.

Bayes. May be, Sir! I'gad, I'm fure on't: *experto crede Roberto.* But I muft give you this caution by the way, be fure you never take † fnuff, when you write.

---

* *If I am to write familiar things,* &c.] This humorous account of Mr. Bayes's management of himfelf, is a banter upon Mr. Dryden's practice, which is alledged to have been much as here reprefented.

† *Be fure you never take fnuff,* &c.] Mr. Dryden was a great taker of fnuff, and made moft of it himfelf.

D 2   *Smi.*

Smi. Why fo, Sir?

Bayes. Why, it fpoil'd me once, I'gad, one of the fparkifheft plays in all England. But a friend of mine at Grefham-College has promis'd to help me to fome fpirit of brains, and I'gad that fhall do my bufinefs.

S C E N E　II.

Enter the two Kings, *hand in hand.*

Bayes. Oh, thefe are now the two kings of Brentford; take notice of their ftile: 'twas never yet upon the ftage; but if you like it, I could make a fhift, perhaps, to fhew you a whole play writ all juft fo.

　1 *King.* Did you obferve their whifpers, bro-
　　ther king?

　2 *King.* I did, and heard befides a grave bird
　　fing,

That they intend, fweet heart, to play us pranks.

Bayes. This is now familiar, becaufe they are both perfons of the fame quality.

Smi. S'death, this would make a man fpew.

　1 *King.* If that defign appears,
　　　　I'll lug 'em by the ears;
　　　　Until I make 'em crack.

　　　　　　　　　　　2 *King.*

2 *King.* And fo will I, i'fack.

1 *King.* You muft begin, *mon foy.*

2 *King.* Sweet Sir, *pardonnez moy:*

Bayes. Mark that: I make 'em both fpeak French to fhew their breeding.

Johnf. O, 'tis extraordinary fine!

2 *King.* Then fpite of fate, we'll thus com-
bined ftand;

And, like true brothers, walk ftill hand in
hand.   [*Exeunt Reges.*

Johnf. This is a majeftic fcene indeed.

Bayes. Ay, 'tis a cruft, a lafting cruft for your rogue-criticks, I'gad; I would fain fee the proud-eft of 'em all but dare to nibble at this; I'gad, if they do, this fhall rub their gums for 'em, I pro-mife you. It was I, you muft know, that have written a whole play juft in this very fame ftile; it was never acted yet.

Johnf. How fo?

Bayes. I'gad, I can hardly tell you, for laugh-ing, ha, ha, ha, it is fo pleafant a ftory: Ha, ha, ha.

Smi. What is't?

Bayes. I'gad the players refus'd to act it. Ha, ha, ha.

Smi. That's impoffible.

D 3   *Bayes.*

53525

Bayes. I'gad they did it, Sir; point-blank re-fus'd it, I'gad, ha, ha, ha.

Johnf. Fie, that was rude.

Bayes. Rude, ay, I'gad they are the rudeft, uncivileft perfons, and all that, in the whole world, I'gad : I'gad, there's no living with 'em : I have written, Mr. Johnfon, I do verily believe, a whole cart-load of things, every whit as good as this, and yet, I vow to gad, thefe infolent rafcals have turn'd 'em all back upon my hands again.

Johnf. Strange fellows, indeed !

Smi. But pray, Mr. Bayes, how came thefe two kings to know of this whifper ! for as I remember, they were not at it.

Bayes. No, but that's the actors fault, and not mine ; for the two kings fhould, a pox take 'em, have popp'd both their heads in at the door, juft as the other went off.

Smi. That, indeed wou'd ha' done it.

Bayes. Done it ! Ay, I'gad, thefe fellows are able to fpoil the beft things in Chriftendom. I'll tell you, Mr. Johnfon, I vow to gad, I have been fo highly difoblig'd by the peremptorinefs of thefe fellows, that I'm refolv'd hereafter to bend my thoughts wholly for the fervice of the nurfery, and mump your proud players, I'gad. So, now

prince

prince Pretty-man comes in, and falls afleep making love to his miftrefs, which, you know, was a grand intrigue in * a late play, written by a very honeft gentleman ; by a knight.

SCENE II.
Enter Prince Pretty-man.

Pret. How ftrange a captive am I grown of late!
 Shall I accufe my love, or blame my fate?
 My love I cannot, that is too divine :
 And againft fate, what mortal dares repine?
  Enter Cloris.

But here fhe comes.
Sure 'tis fome blazing comet! Is it not?

       [*Lies down.*

Bayes. Blazing comet! Mark that, I'gad, very fine !

Pret. But I am fo furpriz'd with fleep, I cannot fpeak the reft.   [*fleeps.*

Bayes. Does not that now furprize you to fall afleep in the nick? His fpirits exhale with the heat of his paffion, and all that, and, fwop, falls afleep as you fee. Now here fhe muft make a fimile.

---

* *In a late play,* &c.] viz. The Loft Lady, wrote by Sir Robert Stapleton.

      Smi.

Smi. Where's the neceffity of that, Mr. Bayes?

Bayes. Becaufe fhe's furpriz'd; that's a general rule; you muft ever make a fimile, when you are furpriz'd; 'tis a new way of writing.

Cloris. * As fome tall pine, which we on Ætna
    find

T'have ftood the rage of many a boift'rous wind;
Feeling without, that flames within do play,
Which would confume his root and fap away;
He fpreads his worfted arms unto the fkies,
Silently grieves, all pale, repines and dies:
So fhrouded up, your bright eye difappears.
Break forth bright fcorching fun, and dry my
    tears.   [*Exit.*

Johnf. Mr. Bayes, methinks, this fimile wants a little application too.

---

† *As fome tall pine,* &c.] In imitation of this paffage.
" As fome fair tulip, by a ftorm oppreft,
" Shrinks up, and folds its filken arms to reft:
" And bending to the blaft, all pale, and dead,
" Hears from within the wind fing round its head:
" So fhrouded up your beauty difappears;
" Unveil, my love, and lay afide your fears.
" The ftorm, that caus'd your fright, is paft and gone."
            Conqueft of Granada, part i. p. 55.
                        Bayes.

Bayes. No, faith; for it alludes to paſſion, to confuming, to dying, and all that; which you know, are the natural effects of an amour. But I'm afraid, this ſcene has made you ſad; for I muſt confeſs, when I writ it, I wept myſelf.

Smi. No truly, Sir, my ſpirits are almoſt exhal'd too, and I am likelier to fall aſleep.

Prince Pretty-man *ſtarts up and ſays——*

Pret. It is reſolv'd. [*Exit.*

Bayes. That's all.

Smi. Mr. Bayes, may one be ſo bold as to aſk you one queſtion now, and you not be angry?

Bayes. O lord, Sir, you may aſk me any thing that you pleaſe; I vow to gad, you do me a great deal of honour: you do not know me, if you ſay that, Sir.

Smi. Then pray, Sir, what is it, that this prince here has reſolv'd in his ſleep?

Bayes. Why, I muſt confeſs, that queſtion is well enough aſk'd, for one that is not acquainted with this new way of writing. But you muſt know, Sir, that to out-do all my fellow writers, whereas they keep their *intrigo* ſecret, till the

very

very laſt ſcene before the dance; I now, Sir, (do you mark me)---a---.

Smi. Begin the play, and end it, without ever opening the plot at all.

Bayes. I do ſo, that's the very plain truth on't ; ha, ha, ha; I do, I'gad. If they cannot find it out themſelves, e'en let 'em alone for Bayes, I warrant you. But here now is a ſcene of buſineſs: pray obſerve it; for I dare ſay you'll think this no unwiſe diſcourſe, nor ill argu'd. To tell you true, 'tis a diſcourſe I over-heard once betwixt two grand, ſober, governing perſons.

S C E N E IV.

Enter Gentleman Uſher *and* Phyſician.

Uſh. Come, Sir, let's ſtate the matter of faƈt, and lay our heads together.

Phyſ. Right, lay our heads together. I love to be merry ſometimes ; but when a knotty point comes, I lay my head cloſe to it, with a ſnuff-box in my hand, and then I fegue it away i'faith.

Bayes. I do juſt ſo, I'gad, always.

Uſh. The grand queſtion is, Whether they heard us whiſper? Which I divide thus.

Phyſ. Yes, it muſt be divided ſo indeed.

Smi.

Smi. That's very complaifant I fwear, Mr. Bayes, to be of another man's opinion, before he knows what it is.

Bayes. Nay, I bring in none here but well bred perfons, I affure you.

Ufh. I divide the queftion into when they heard, what they heard, and whether they heard or no.

Johnf. Moft admirably divided, I fwear!

Ufh. As to the when; you fay juft now: fo that is anfwered. Then as for what; why, what anfwers itfelf; for what could they hear, but what we talk'd of? fo that naturally, and of neceffity, we come to the laft queftion, *viz.* Whether they heard or no?

Smi. This is a very wife fcene, Mr. Bayes.

Bayes. Ay, you have it right; they are both politicians.

Ufh. Pray then, to proceed in method, let me afk you that queftion.

Phyf. No you'll anfwer better, pray let me afk it you.

Ufh. Your will muft be a law.

Phyf. Come then, what is't I muft afk?

Smi. This politician, I perceive, Mr. Bayes, has fomewhat a fhort memory.

Bayes.

Bayes. Why, Sir, you muſt know, that t'other is the main politician, and this is but his pupil.

Uſh. You muſt aſk me whether they heard us whiſper.

Phyſ. Well I do ſo.

Uſh. Say it then.

Smi. Hey day! here's the braveſt work that ever I ſaw.

Johnſ. This is mighty methodical!

Bayes. Ay, Sir; that's the way, 'tis the way of art; there is no other way, I'gad, in buſineſs.

Phyſ. Did they hear us whiſper?

Uſh. Why, truly, I can't tell; there's much to be ſaid upon the word whiſper; to whiſper, in *Latin* is *ſuſurrare,* which is as much as to ſay, to ſpeak ſoftly; now, if they heard us ſpeak ſoftly, they heard us whiſper: but then comes in the *quomodo,* the how; how did they hear us whiſper? Why, as to that, there are two ways; the one by chance or accident, the other on purpoſe; that is, with deſign to hear us whiſper.

Phyſ. Nay, if they heard us that way, I'll never give 'em phyſick more.

Uſh. Nor I e'er more will walk abroad before 'em.

Bayes.

Bayes. Pray mark this: for a great deal depends upon it, towards the latter end of the play.

Smi. I suppose, that's the reason why you brought in this scene, Mr. Bayes.

Bayes. Partly it was, Sir; but I confess, I was not unwilling besides, to shew the world a pattern here, how men should talk of business.

Johns. You have done it exceeding well indeed.

Bayes. Yes, I think, this will do.

Phys. Well, if they heard us whisper, they'll turn us out, and no body else will take us.

Smi. Not for politicians, I dare answer for it.

Phys. Let's then no more ourselves in vain be-
                moan:
We are not safe until we them unthrone.

Ush. 'Tis right:
And since occasion now seems debonair,
I'll seize on this, and you shall take that chair.
[*They draw their swords, and sit in the two great
            chairs upon the stage.*]

Bayes. There's now an odd surprize*; the

* *The whole state's turn'd quite topsie turvy, &c.*] Such easy turns of state are frequent in our modern plays; where we see princes dethron'd, and governments changed, by very feeble means, and on slight occasions: particu-
                                larly,

whole ſtate's turn'd quite topſie-turvy, without any pother or ſtir in the whole world.

larly, in Marriage A-la-Mode ; a play, wrote ſince the firſt publication of this farce. Where (to paſs by the dulneſs of the ſtate-part, the obſcurity of the comic, the near re-ſemblance Leonidas bears to our prince Pretty-man, being ſometimes a king's ſon, ſometimes a ſhepherd's ; and, not to queſtion how Amalthea comes to be a princeſs, her brother, the king's great favourite, being but a lord) 'tis worth our while to obſerve, how eaſily the fierce and jea-lous uſurper is depos'd, and the right heir plac'd on the throne : as it is thus related by the ſaid imaginary prin-ceſs.

" *Amal.* Oh, gentlemen, if you have loyalty,
" Or courage, ſhew it now : Leonidas,
" Broke on a ſudden from his guards, and ſnatching
" A ſword from one, his back againſt the ſcaffold,
" Bravely defends himſelf ; and owns aloud
" He is our long loſt king, found for this moment ;
" But if your valours help not, loſt for ever.
" Two of his guards, mov'd by the ſenſe of virtue,
" Are turn'd for him ; and there they ſtand at bay,
" Againſt a hoſt of foes." *Marriage d-la-Mode*, p. 69.

This ſhews Mr. Bayes to be a man of conſtancy, and firm to his reſolution, and not to be laugh'd out of his own method : agreeable to what he ſays in the next act.

" As long as I know my things are good, what care I
" what they ſay ?"

Johnſ.

Johnf. A very filent change of government, truly, as ever I heard of.

Bayes. It is fo. And yet you fhall fee me bring 'em in again, by and by, in as odd a way every jot.

[*The ufurpers march out flourifhing their fwords.*]

Enter Shirley.

Shir. Hey ho, hey ho; what a change is here*! hey day! hey day! I know not what to do, nor what to fay,   [*Exit.*

Johnf. Mr. Bayes, in my opinion, now, that gentleman might have faid a little more upon this occafion.

Bayes. No, Sir, not at all; for I underwrit his part, on purpofe to fet off the reft.

Johnf. Cry you mercy, Sir.

Smi. But pray, Sir, how came they to depofe the kings fo eafily?

* *Hey day, hey day! I know not what to do, nor what to fay.*]

" I know not what to fay, nor what to think :
" I know not when I fleep, nor when I wake."
       Love and Friendfhip, p. 46.

" My doubts and fears my reafon do difmay.
" I know not what to do, nor what to fay."
       Pandora, p. 46.
       Bayes.

Bayes. Why, Sir, you muſt know, they long had a deſign to do it before; but never could put it in practice till now; and to tell you true, that's one reaſon why I made 'em whiſper ſo at firſt.

Smi. O, very well, now I am fully ſatisfy'd.

Bayes. And then to ſhew you, Sir, it was not done ſo very eaſily neither, in the next ſcene you ſhall ſee ſome fighting.

Smi. O, oh, ſo then you make the ſtruggle to be after the buſineſs is done.

Bayes. Ay.

Smi. O, I conceive you; that, I ſwear, is very natural.

S C E N E V.

Enter four men at one door, and four at another, with their ſwords drawn.

1 *Soldier.* Stand: Who goes there?

2 *Sol.* A friend.

1 *Sol.* What friend?

2 *Sol.* A friend to the houſe.

1 *Sol.* Fall on.   [*They all kill one another.*
            [*Muſic ſtrikes.*

Bayes. Hold, hold,   [*To the muſic. It ceaſeth.*
Now, here's an odd ſurprize; all theſe dead men

1   you

you shall see rise up presently, at a certain note
that I have made, in *Effaut flat*, and fall a dancing. Do you hear dead men? Remember your
note in *Effaut flat*.

Play on.   [*To the musick.*

Now, now, now!

[*The musick plays his note, and the dead men rise;
but cannot get in order.*

O lord! O lord!

Out, out, out! Did ever men spoil a good thing
so? no figure, no ear, no time, no thing! Ud-
zookers, you dance worse than the angels in Harry
the Eighth, or the fat spirits in the Tempest.

  1 *Sol.* Why, Sir, 'tis impossible to do any thing
in time to this tune.

  Bayes. O lord, O lord, impossible! Why, gentlemen, if there be any faith in a person that's a
christian, I sate up two whole nights in composing
this air, and adapting it for the business: For if you
observe, there are two several designs in this tune;
it begins swift, and ends slow. You talk of time
and time; you shall see me do't: Look you now.
Here I am dead.

           [*Lies down flat on his face.*

Vol. I.   E   Now,

Now, mark my note *Effaut flat*. Strike up mufick. Now,

      [*As he rifes up haftily, he falls down again.*
Ah, gadzookers, I have broke my nofe.

Johnf. By my troth, Mr. Bayes, this is a very
unfortunate note of yours, in *Effaut.*

Bayes. A plague of this damn'd ftage, with your
nails and tenter-hooks, that a gentleman cannot
come to teach you to act, but he muft break his
nofe and his face, and the devil and all. Pray, Sir,
can you help me to a wet piece of brown paper?

Smi. No, indeed, Sir, I don't ufually carry any
about me.

2 Sol. Sir, I'll go get you fome within prefently.

Bayes. Go, go then ; I follow you. Pray dance
out the dance, and I'll be with you in a moment.
Remember you dance like horfemen.

Smi. Like horfemen! what a plague can that
be.   [*Exit* Bayes.

[*They dance the dance, but can make nothing of it.*

1 Sol. A devil! let's try this no longer : play
my dance that Mr. Bayes found fault with fo.

                [*Dance and exeunt.*
                         Smi.

Smi. What can this fool be doing all this while about his nofe ?

Johnf. Pr'ythee, let's go fee.

END OF THE SECOND ACT.

ACT III.   SCENE I.

Bayes, *with a paper on his nofe, and the two gentlemen.*

Bayes. Now, Sirs, this I do, becaufe my fancy, in this play, is to end every act with a dance.

Smi. Faith, that fancy is very good; but I fhould hardly have broke my nofe for it tho'.

Johnf. That fancy, I fuppofe, is new too.

Bayes. Sir, all my fancies are fo. I tread upon no man's heels; but make my flight upon my own wings, I affure you. *Now, here comes in a fcene of fheer wit, without any mixture in the whole world, I'gad---between prince Pretty-man

* *Now, here comes in a fcene of fheer wit, &c.*] This defcription of the following fcene betwixt Prince Pretty-man and Tom Thimble, his taylor, and the fcene itfelf, is an admirable fatyr, and parody on the fcene betwixt Failer and Bibber, his taylor, in the Wild Gallant, p. 5 & 6.

E 2   and

and his taylor: it might properly enough be called a prize of wit; for you ſhall ſee 'em come in upon one another ſnip ſnap, hit for hit, as faſt as can be. Firſt one ſpeaks, then preſently t'other's upon him, flap, with a repartee, then he at him again, daſh with a new conceit; and ſo eternally, eternally, I'gad, till they go quite off the ſtage.

[*Goes to call the players.*

Smi. What a plague does this fop mean by his ſnip ſnap, hit for hit, and daſh?

Johnſ. Mean! why, he never meant any thing in's life: what do'ſt talk of meaning for?

Enter Bayes.

Bayes. Why don't you come in?

Enter Prince Pretty-man *and* Tom Thimble.
This ſcene will make you die with laughing, if it be well acted; for it is as full of drollery as ever it can hold. 'Tis like an orange ſtuff'd with cloves, as for conceit.

Pret. But pr'ythee, Tom Thimble, why wilt thou needs marry? If nine taylors make but one man; and one woman cannot be ſatisfied with nine men; what work art thou cutting out here for thyſelf, trow?

Bayes. Good.

2

Thim.

Thim. Why, an't pleafe your highnefs, if I can't make up all the work I cut out, I fhan't want journeymen enough to help me, I warrant you.

Bayes. Good again.

Pret. I am afraid thy journeymen tho', Tom, won't work by the day, but by the night.

Bayes. Good ftill.

Thim. However, if my wife fits but crofs-legg'd, as I do, there will be no great danger; not half fo much as when I trufted you, Sir, for your coronation-fuit.

Bayes. Very good i'faith.

Pret. Why, the times then liv'd upon truft; it was the fafhion. You would not be out of time, at fuch a time, as that, fure : A taylor, you know, muft never be out of fafhion.

Bayes. Right.

Thim. *I'm fure, Sir, I made your cloaths in the court-fafhion, for you never paid me yet.

Bayes. There's a bob for the court.

Pret. Why, Tom, thou'rt a fharp rogue when

* *I'm fure I made your cloaths,* &c.] " Nay, if that be " all, there's no fuch hafte. The courtiers are not fo for- " ward to pay their debts." *Wild Gallant,* p. 9.

E 3   thou

thou art angry, I fee: thou pay'ſt me now, methinks.

Bayes. There's pay upon pay, as good as ever
was written.

Thim. *Ay, Sir, in your own coin: you give
me nothing but words.

Bayes. Admirable, ~~before gad!~~

Pret. Well, Tom, I hope ſhortly I ſhall have
another coin for thee; for now the wars are coming on, I ſhall grow to be a man of metal.

Bayes. O, you did not do that half enough.

Johnſ. Methinks he does it admirably.

Bayes. Ay, pretty well; but he does not hit
me in't: †he does not top his part.

---

* *Ay, Sir, in your own coin, you give me nothing but
words.*]

  " *Failer.* Take a little Bibber,
  " And throw him in the river,
  " And if he will truſt never,
  " Then there let him lie ever.
  " *Bibber.* Then ſay I,
  " Take a little Failer,
  " And throw him to the jailor,
  " And there let him lie,
  " Till he has paid his taylor." *Wild Gall.* p. 12.

† *He does not top his part.*] To top a part was a great
word with Mr. *Edward Howard.*

           Thim.

Thim. That's the way to be ftamp'd yourfelf, Sir. I fhall fee you come home, like an angel for the king's evil, with a hole bor'd thro' you.

[*Exeunt.*

Bayes. Ha, there he has hit it up to the hilts, I'gad! How do you like it now, gentlemen? is not this pure wit?

Smi. 'Tis fnip fnap, Sir, as you fay; but me-thinks, not pleafant, nor to the purpofe, for the play does not go on.

Bayes. Play does not go on! I don't know what you mean! why, is not this part of the play?

Smi. Yes, but the plot ftands ftill.

Bayes. Plot ftands ftill! why, what a devil is the plot good for, but to bring in fine things?

Smi. O, I did not know that before.

Bayes. No, I think you did not; nor many things more that I am mafter of. Now, Sir, I'gad, this is the bane of all us writers; let us foar but never fo little above the common pitch, I'gad, all's fpoil'd, for the vulgar never underftand it; they can never conceive you, Sir, the excellency of thefe things.

Johnf.

Johnf. 'Tis a fad fate, I muſt confeſs ; but you write on ſtill for all that ?

Bayes. Write on! Ay, I'gad, I warrant you. 'Tis not their talk ſhall ſtop me; if they catch me at that lock, I'll give 'em leave to hang me. * As long as I know my things are good, what care I what they ſay ? what, are they gone, without finging my laſt new ſong ? 'Sbud, would it were in their bellies. I'll tell you, Mr. Johnſon, if I have any ſkill in theſe matters, I vow to gad, this ſong is peremptorily the very beſt that ever yet was written: you muſt know, it was made by Tom Thimble's firſt wife after ſhe was dead.

Smi. How, Sir, after ſhe was dead ?

Bayes. Ay, Sir, after ſhe was dead. Why, what have you to ſay to that ?

Johnf. Say ? Why nothing: he were a devil, that had any thing to ſay to that.

Bayes. Right.

Smi. How did ſhe come to die, pray, Sir.

* *As long as I know my things are good, what care I what they ſay.*] Referring to Mr. Dryden's obſtinate adhe-rence to ſome things in his plays, in oppoſition to the ſound judgment of all unprejudic'd Critics. See an in-ſtance of this noticed in the note, p. 178.

Bayes.

Bayes. Phoo! that's no matter; by a fall; but here's the conceit, that, upon his knowing fhe was killed by an accident, he fuppofes, with a figh, that fhe died for love of him.

Johnf. Ay, ay, that's well enough: let's hear it, Mr. Bayes.

Bayes. 'Tis to the tune of, Farewel, fair Armida, on feas, and in battles, in bullets, and all that.

S O N G.

* In fwords, pikes, and bullets, 'tis fafer to be,
Than in a ftrong caftle, remoted from thee:

* *In fwords, pikes, and bullets*, &c.] In imitation of this paffage,

" On feas, and in battles, thro' bullets and fire,
" The danger is lefs, than in hopelefs defire;
" My death's wound you gave me, tho' far off I bear
" My fall from your fight, not to coft you a tear;
" But if the kind flood on a wave would convey,
" And under your window my body would lay;
" When the wound on my breaft you happen to fee,
" You'll fay, with a figh, it was given by me."

This is the latter part of a fong made by Mr. Bayes, on the death of captain Digby, fon of George earl of Briftol, who was a paffionate admirer of the dutchefs dowager of Richmond, called by the author, Armida; he loft his life in a fea-fight againft the Dutch, the 28th of May, 1672.

My

My death's bruife pray think you gave me, tho'
    a fall
Did give it me more, from the top of a wall ;
For then if the moat, on her mud would firft
    lay,
And after, before you my body convey :
The blue on my breaft when you happen to fee,
  You'll fay, with a figh, there's a true blue
    for me.

Ha, rogues! when I am merry, I write thefe
things as faft as hops, I'gad ; for you muft know
I am as pleafant a debauchee as ever you faw, I
am i'faith.

Smi. But, Mr. Bayes, how comes this fong in
here ? for, methinks, there is no great occafion
for it.

Bayes. Alack, Sir, you know nothing, you
muft ever interlard your plays with fongs, ghofts,
and dances, if you mean to—a—

Johnf. * Pit, box, and gallery it, Mr. Bayes.

Bayes. I'gad and you have nick'd it. Hark
you, Mr. Johnfon, you know I don't flatter ;
I'gad you have a great deal of wit.

---

* *Pit, box, and gallery it, Mr. Bayes.*] Mr. Edward
Howard's cant-words. See note upon p. 10.

                    Johnf.

Johnf. O lord, Sir, you do me too much honour.

Bayes. Nay, nay, come, come, Mr. Johnfon, i'faith, this muft not be faid amongft us that have it. I know you have wit by the judgment you make of this play; for that's the meafure I go by; my play is my touchftone. When a man tells me fuch a one is a perfon of parts! Is he fo, fays I? What do I do, but bring him prefently to fee this play; if he likes it, I know what to think of him; if not, your muft humble fervant, Sir; I'll no more of him, upon my word, I thank you. I am *Clara voyant*, I'gad. Now, here we go on to our bufinefs.

S C E N E II.

Enter the two ufurpers, hand in hand.

Ufh. But what's become of Volfcius the great?
    His prefence has not grac'd our court of late.
Phyf. I fear fome ill, from emulation fprung,
    Has from us that illuftrious hero wrung.
Bayes. Is not that majeftical?
Smi. Yes, but who the devil is this Volfcius?
Bayes. Why, that's a prince I make in love with Parthenope.
Smi. I thank you, Sir.

Enter

Enter Cordelio.

* *Cor.* My lieges, news from Volſcius the prince.

Uſh. His news is welcome, whatſoe'er it be.

Smi. How, Sir, do you mean whether it be good or bad?

Bayes. Nay, pray, Sir, have a little patience: gadzookers, you'll ſpoil all my play. Why, Sir, 'tis impoſſible to anſwer every impertinent queſtion you aſk.

Smi. Cry you mercy, Sir.

Cor. His highneſs, Sirs, commanded me to
 tell you,

That the fair perſon whom you both do know,

Deſpairing of forgiveneſs for her fault,

In a deep ſorrow, twice ſhe did attempt

Upon her precious life; but, by the care

Of ſtanders-by prevented was.

Smi. 'Sheart, what ſtuff's here?

Cor. At laſt,

* *Cor. My lieges, news from Volſcius the prince.*
Uſh. His news is welcome, whatſoe'er it be.]
" *Albert.* Curtius, I've ſomething to deliver to your ear.
" *Curt.* Any thing from Alberto is welcome."

Amorous Prince, p. 39.

Volſcius

Volſcius the great this dire reſolve embrac'd:
His ſervants he into the country ſent,
And he himſelf to Peccadilla went,
Where he's inform'd, by letters, that ſhe's dead.

Uſh. Dead! is that poſſible? Dead!

Phyſ. O ye gods!

Bayes. There's a ſmart expreſſion of a paſſion; O ye gods! That's one of my bold ſtrokes, I'gad.

Smi. Yes; who is the fair perſon that's dead?

Bayes. That you ſhall know anon, Sir!

Smi. Nay, if we know at all, 'tis well enough.

Bayes. Perhaps you may find too, by and by, for all this, that ſhe's not dead neither.

Smi. Marry, that's good news indeed: I am glad of that with all my heart.

Bayes. Now, here's the man brought in that is ſuppoſed to have kill'd her. [*A great ſhout within.*

. S C E N E III.

Enter Amaryllis, *with a book in her hand, and attendants.*

Ama. What ſhout triumphant's that?

Enter a Soldier.

Sol. Shy maid, upon the river brink, near Twic'nam town, the falſe aſſaſſinate is ta'en.

Ama.

Ama. Thanks to the powers above, for this de-
liverance.   I hope,
Its flow beginning will portend
A forward exit to all future end.

Bayes. Pifh, there you are out; to all future
end? No, no; to all future end! You muft lay
the accent upon end, or elfe you lofe the conceit.

Smi. I fee you are very perfect in thefe matters.

Bayes. Ay, Sir, I have been long enough at it,
one would think, to know fomething.

Enter Soldiers, dragging an old fifherman.

Ama. Villain, what monfter did corrupt thy
    mind,
    T' attack the nobleft foul of human kind;
    Tell me who fet thee on.

Fifh. Prince Pretty-man.

Ama. To kill whom?

Fifh. Prince Pretty-man.

Ama. What, did Prince Pretty-man hire you to
kill Prince Pretty-man?

Fifh. No; Prince Volfcius.

Ama. To kill whom?

Fifh. Prince Volfcius.

Ama. What, did Prince Volfcius hire you to
kill Prince Volfcius?

                          Fifh.

Fiſh. No, Prince Pretty-man.

Ama. So, drag him hence,

Till torture of the rack produce his ſenſe.

[Exeunt.

Bayes. Mark, how I make the horror of his guilt confound his intellects; for he's out at one and t'other: and that's the deſign of this ſcene.

Smi. I ſee, Sir, you have a ſeveral deſign for every ſcene.

Bayes. Ay, that's my way of writing; and ſo, Sir, I can diſpatch you a whole Play before another man, I'gad, can make an end of his plot.

<h2 align="center">S C E N E IV.</h2>

Bayes. So now enter Prince Pretty-man in a rage. Where the devil is he? Why Pretty-man? why when, I ſay? O fie! fie! fie! fie! all's marr'd, I vow to gad, quite marr'd.

Enter Pretty-man.

Phoo pox! you are come too late, Sir; now you may go out again, if you pleaſe. I vow to gad, Mr.---a---I would not give a button for my play, now you have done this.

Pret. What, Sir?

Bayes. What, Sir! 'ſlife, Sir, you ſhould have

come

come out in choler, rouze upon the ſtage, juſt as the other went off. Muſt a man be eternally telling you of theſe things?

Johnſ. Sure this muſt be ſome very notable matter that he's ſo angry at.

Smi. I am not of your opinion.

Bayes. Piſh! come let's hear your part, Sir.

Pret. Bring in my father; why d'ye keep him from me?

Altho' a fiſher-man, he is my father:
Was ever ſon, yet brought to this diſtreſs,
To be, for being a ſon, made fatherleſs?
Ah, you juſt gods, rob me not of a father:
The being of a ſon take from me rather.

Smi. Well, Ned, what think you now?

Johnſ. A devil, this is worſt of all. Mr. Bayes, pray what's the meaning of this ſcene?

Bayes. O, cry you mercy, Sir: I proteſt I had forgot to tell you. Why, Sir, you muſt know, that long before the beginning of this play, this prince was taken by a fiſherman.

Smi. How, Sir, taken priſoner.

Bayes. Taken priſoner! O lord, what a queſtion's there! did ever any man aſk ſuch a queſtion? Gadzookers, he has put the plot quite out of my
head,

head, with this damn'd queſtion. What was I going to ſay?

Johnſ. Nay, the lord knows: I cannot imagine.

Bayes. Stay, let me ſee; taken: O 'tis true. Why, Sir, as I was going to ſay, his highneſs here, the prince, was taken in a cradle by a fiſherman, and brought up as his child.

Smi. Indeed!

Bayes. Nay, pr'ythee hold thy peace. And ſo Sir, this murder being committed by the river-ſide, the fiſherman upon ſuſpicion, was ſeiz'd, and thereupon the prince grew angry.

Smi. So, ſo; now 'tis very plain.

Johnſ. But, Mr. Bayes, is not this ſome diſparagement to a prince, to paſs for a fiſherman's ſon? Have a care of that, I pray.

Bayes. No, no, not at all; for 'tis but for a while: I ſhall fetch him off again preſently, you ſhall ſee.

Enter Pretty-man *and* Thimble.

Pret. By all the gods, I'll ſet the world on fire,
 Rather then let 'em raviſh hence my fire.

Thim. Brave Pretty-man, it is at length reveal'd.
 That he is not thy fire who thee conceal'd.

Bayes. Lo'you now; there he's off again.

Johnſ.

Johnf. Admirably done i'faith.

Bayes. Ay, now the plot thickens very much upon us.

Pret. What oracle this darknefs can evince?
Sometimes a fifher's fon, fometimes a prince.
It is a fecret, great as is the world;
In which I, like the foul, am tofs'd and hurl'd.
The blackeft ink of fate, fure was my lot,
And when fhe writ my name, fhe made a blot.
                                        [*Exit.*

Bayes. There's a bluftering verfe for you now.

Smi. Yes, Sir; but why is he fo mightily troubled to find he is not a fifherman's fon?

Bayes. Phoo! that is not becaufe he has a mind to be his fon, but for fear he fhould be thought to be no bodies fon at all.

Smi. Nay, that would trouble a man indeed.

Bayes. So, let me fee.

SCENE V.

Enter Prince Volfcius, *going out of town.*

Smi. I thought he had been gone to Piccadilly.

Bayes. Yes he gave it out fo : but that was only to cover his defign.

Johnf. What defign?

                                        Bayes.

Bayes. Why to head the army, that lies concealed for him at Knights-bridge.

Johnf. I fee here's a great deal of plot, Mr. Bayes.

Bayes. Yes, now it begins to break; but we fhall have a world of more bufinefs anon.

Enter Prince Volfcius, Cloris, Amaryllis, *and* Harry *with a riding cloak and boots.*

Ama. Sir, you are cruel, thus to leave the town,
And to retire to country folitude.

Clo. We hop'd this fummer that we fhould at leaft
Have held the honour of your company.

Bayes. Held the honour of your company; prettily expreft, held the honour of your company! Gadzookers, thefe fellows will never take notice of any thing.

Johnf. I affure you, Sir, I admire it extremely: I don't know what he does.

Bayes. Ay, ay, he's a little envious; but 'tis no great matter. Come.

Ama. Pray let us two this fingle boon obtain,
    That you will here, with poor us, ftill remain.
    Before your horfes come, pronounce our fate,
    For then, alas! I fear 'twill be too late.

Bayes.

Bayes. Sad!

Vol. *Harry, my boots; for I'll range among
    My blades encamp'd, and quit this urban
      throng.

Smi. But pray, Mr. Bayes, is not this a little difficult, that you were saying e'en now, to keep an army thus conceal'd in Knights-bridge?

Bayes. In Knights-bridge? stay.

Johnf. No, not if inn-keepers be his friends.

Bayes. His friends! Ay, Sir, his intimate acquaintance; or elfe indeed I grant it could not be.

Smi. Yes, faith, fo it might be very eafy.

Bayes. Nay, if I do not make all things eafy, I'gad, I'll give you leave to hang me. Now you would think that he's going out of town; but you fhall fee how prettily I have contriv'd to ftop him prefently.

* *Harry my boots,* &c.] In imitation of the following paffage.

  " Let my horfes be brought ready to the door, for I'll
" go out of town this evening."

    " Into the country I'll with fpeed,
    " With hounds and hawks my fancy feed, &c."
    " Now I'll away, a country life
    " Shall be my miftrefs, and my wife."

               Englifh Monfeur, p. 36, 38, 39.

Smi. By my troth, Sir, you have so amaz'd me
that I know not what to think.

Enter Parthenope.

Volf. Blefs me! how frail are all my best resolves!
How, in a moment, is my purpose chang'd!
Too foon I thought myself fecure from love.
   * Fair madam, give me leave to ask her name,
Who does fo gently rob me of my fame?
For I should meet the army out of town,
And if I fail, must hazard my renown.

Par. My mother, Sir, fells ale by the town-walls,
    And me her dear Parthenope she calls.

Bayes. Now that's the Parthenope, I told you of.

Johns. Ay, ay, I'gad, you are very right.

Volf. Can vulgar vestments high-born beauty
      shroud?
    † Thou bring'st the morning pictur'd in a
      cloud.

Bayes. The morning pictur'd in a cloud! Ah,
gadzookers, what a conceit is there!

---

  * *Fair madam, give me leave to ask her name.*] " And
" what's this maids name?"   *English Monfieur*, p. 40.
  † *Thou bring'st the morning pictur'd in a cloud.*] " I
" bring the morning pictur'd in a cloud."
                Siege of Rhodes, part 1. p. 10.

Par. Give you good even, Sir.

Volf. O inaufpicious ftars! that I was born

　　To fudden love, and to more fudden fcorn.

Ama.⎱ *How! prince Volfcius in love? Ha,
Clo.⎰ ha, ha.　　　　　　[*Exeunt laughing.*

Smi. Sure, Mr. Bayes, we have loft fome jeft
here, that they laugh at fo.

Bayes. Why, did you not obferve? he firft re-
folves to go out of town, and then, as he is pul-
ling on his boots, falls in love with her, ha, ha, ha.

Smi. Well, and where lies the jeft of that?

Bayes. Ha!　　　　　　　　　[*Turns to* Johnf.

Johnf. Why, in the boots, where fhould the
jeft lie?

Bayes. I'gad, you are in the right; it does

　　　　　　　　　　[*Turns to* Smith.
Lie in the boots-------Your friend, and I know
where a good jeft lies, tho' you don't, Sir.

Smi. Much good do't you, Sir.

Bayes. Here now, Mr. Johnfon; you fhall fee
a combat betwixt love and honour.　† An ancient

　* *How! prince Volcius in love?*]
　" Mr. Comely in love!"　　*Englifh Monfieur*, p. 49.

　† *An ancient author has made a whole play on't.*] The
play alluded to is, Sir William Davenant's play of Love
and Honour.

　　　　　　　　　　　　　　author

author has made a whole play o'nt; but I have difpatch'd it all in this fcene.

Volfcius *fits down to pull on his boots:* Bayes *ftands by, and over-aĉts the part as he fpeaks it.*

Volf. How has my paffion made me Cupid's fcoff?
This hafty boot is on, the other off,
And fullen lies, with amorous defign
To quit loud fame, and make that beauty
mine.

Smi. Pr'ythee mark what pains Mr. Bayes takes to aĉt this fpeech himfelf!

Johnf. Yes, the fool, I fee, is mightily tranfported with it.

Volf. My legs, the emblem of my various
. thought,
Shew to what fad diftraĉtion I am brought.
Sometimes with ftubborn honour, like this
boot,
My mind is guarded, and refolv'd to do't:
Sometimes, again, that very mind, by love
Difarm'd, like this other leg does prove.
Shall I to honour, or to love give way?
*Go on, cries honour; tender love fays nay:

* *Go on, cries honour,* &c.] In imitation of " But " honour fays not fo." *Siege of* Rhodes, part. 1. p. 19.

Honour

Honour aloud commands, pluck both boots
    on;
But softer love does whisper, put on none;
What shall I do? what conduct shall I find
To lead me thro' this twilight of my mind?
For as bright day, with black approach of
    night
Contending, makes a doubtful puzzling light?
So does my honour and my love together
Puzzle me so, I can resolve for neither.

[*Goes out hopping with one boot on, and the other off.*

Johns. By my troth, Sir, this is as difficult a
combat as ever I saw, and as equal; for 'tis determin'd on neither side.

Bayes. Ay, is't not now, I'gad, ha? For to go
off hip-hop, hip-hop upon this occasion, is a thousand times better than any conclusion in the
world, I'gad.

Johns. Indeed, Mr. Bayes, that hip-hop, in this
place as you say, does a very great deal.

Bayes. O, all in all, Sir, they are these little
things that mar, or set you off a play; * as I remember once in a play of mine, I set off a scene,

---

* *As I remember once,* &c.] The play here hinted at is,
Mr. Dryden's Love in a Nunnery, p. 34.

I'gad,

I'gad, beyond expectation, only with a petticoat, and the belly-ach.

Smi. Pray how was that, Sir?

Bayes. Why, Sir, I contriv'd a petticoat to be brought in upon a chair, (no body knew how) into a prince's chamber, whofe father was not to fee but that it came in by chance.

Johnf. Gad's-my-life, that was a notable contrivance indeed.

Smi. Ay, but, Mr. Bayes, how could you contrive the belly-ach?

Bayes. The eafieft i'th' world, I'gad; I'll tell you how, I made the prince fit down upon the petticoat, no more than fo, and pretend to his father that he had juft then got the belly-ach: whereupon his father went out to call a phyfician, and his man run away with the petticoat.

Smi. Well, and what follow'd upon that?

Bayes. Nothing, no earthly thing, I vow.

Johnf. O' my-word, Mr. Bayes, there you hit it.

Bayes. Yes it gave a world of content. And then I paid 'em away befides; for I made 'em all talk baudry; ha, ha, ha, beaftly, down-right baudry

baudry upon the ftage, I'gad, ha, ha, ha; but with an infinite deal of wit, that I muft fay.

Johnf That, we know well enough, can never fail you.

Bayes. No, that can't it.   Come, bring in the dance.   [*Exit to call the players.*

Smi. Now the devil take thee for a filly, confident, unnatural, fulfome rogue.

Enter Bayes *and* Players.

Bayes. Pray dance well before the gentlemen : you are commonly fo lazy; but you fhould be light and eafy, tah, tah, tah.

[*All the while they dance,*
Bayes *puts 'em out with teaching 'em.*
Well, gentlemen, you'll fee this dance, if I am not deceiv'd, take very well upon the ftage, when they are perfect in their motions, and all that.

Smi. I don't know how 'twill take, Sir; but I am fure you fweat hard for't.

Bayes. Ay, Sir, it cofts me more pains and trouble to do thefe things, than almoft the things are worth.

Smi. By my troth, I think fo, Sir.

Bayes.

Bayes. Not for the things themſelves; for I could write you, Sir, forty of 'em in a day; but, I'gad, theſe players are ſuch dull perſons, that if a man be not by 'em upon every point, and at every turn, I'gad, they'll miſtake you, Sir, and ſpoil all.

Enter a Player.

.What! is the funeral ready?

Play. Yes, Sir.

Bayes. And is the lance fill'd with wine?

Play. Sir, 'tis juſt now a-doing.

Bayes. Stay then, I'll do it myſelf.

Smi. Come, let's go with him.

Bayes. A match: but, Mr. Johnſon, I'gad, I am not like other perſons, they care not what be- comes of their things, ſo they can but get money for 'em; now, I'gad, when I write, if it be not juſt as it ſhould be in every circumſtance, to every particular, I'gad, I am no more able to endure it; I am not myſelf, I'm out of my wits, and all that; I'm the ſtrangeſt perſon in the whole world : For what care I for money ? I write for reputation.

[*Exeunt.*

END OF THE THIRD ACT.

ACT IV. SCENE I.

Bayes, and two gentlemen.

Bayes. GEntlemen, becaufe I would not have any two things alike in this play, the laft act beginning with a witty fcene of mirth, I make this to begin with a funeral.

Smi. And is that all your reafon for it, Mr. Bayes?

Bayes. No, Sir, I have a precedent for it befides. * A perfon of honour, and a fcholar, brought in his funeral juft fo: and he was one, let me tell you, that knew as well what belong'd to a funeral, as any man in England, I'gad.

Johnf. Nay if that be fo, you are fafe.

Bayes. I'gad, but I have another device, a frolick, which I think yet better than all this; not for the plot or characters, (for in my heroick plays, I make no difference as to thofe matters) but for another contrivance.

---

* *A perfon of honour*, &c.] Col. Henry Howard begun his play, called *The United Kingdoms*, with a funeral. *vid.* the note at p. 18.

Smi.

Smi. What is that, I pray?

Bayes. Why, I have defign'd a conqueft, that cannot poffibly, I'gad, be acted in lefs than a whole week : * and I'll fpeak a bold word ; it fhall drum, trumpet, fhout and battle, I'gad, with any the moft warlike tragedy we have, either ancient or modern.

Johnf. Ay marry, Sir, there you fay fomething.

Smi. And pray, Sir, how have you order'd this fame frolick of yours ?

Bayes. Faith, Sir, by the rule of romance. For example, they divided their things into three, four, five, fix, feven, eight, or as many tomes as they pleafed : now I would very fain know, what fhould hinder me from doing the fame with my things, if I pleafe ?

Johnf. Nay, if you fhould not be a mafter of your own works, 'tis very hard.

Bayes. That is my fenfe: and then, Sir, this contrivance of mine has fomething of the reafon of a play in it too ; for as every one makes you

---

* *And I'll fpeak a bold word ; it fhall drum, &c.*] Thefe are Mr. Dryden's words in his preface to the Conqueft of Granada.

five acts to one play,* what do I, but make five plays to one plot ; by which means the auditors have every day a new thing.

Johnf. Moſt admirably good, i'faith ! and muſt certainly take, becauſe it is not tedious.

Bayes. Ay, Sir, I know that, there's the main point.   And then upon Saturday to make a cloſe of all, (for I ever begin upon a Monday) I make you, Sir, a ſixth play, that ſums up the whole matter to 'em, and all that, for fear they ſhould have forgot it.

Johnf. That conſideration, Mr. Bayes, indeed I think will be very neceſſary.

Smi. And when comes in your ſhare pray, Sir ?

Bayes. The third week.

Johnf. I'll vow you'll get a world of money.

Bayes. Why, i'faith, a man muſt live : and if you don't thus pitch upon ſome new device, I'gad, you'll never do't ; for this age (take it o'my word) is ſomewhat hard to pleaſe.   But there's one pretty odd paſſage in the laſt of theſe plays,

---

* *What do I, but make five plays to one plot ?*] Alluding to Mr. Dryden's practice of dividing his plots among ſeveral plays, as in the Conqueſt of Granada, I. and II. parts.   Indian Emperor and Indian Queen, &c.

which

which may be executed two feveral ways, wherein I'd have your opinion, gentlemen.

Johnf. What is't, Sir?

Bayes. Why, Sir, I make a male perfon to be in love with a female.

Smi. Do you mean that, Mr. Bayes, for a new thing?

Bayes. Yes, Sir, as I have order'd it. You fhall hear: he having paffionately lov'd her through my five whole plays, finding at laft that fhe confents to his love, juft after that his mother had appear'd to him like a ghoft, he kills himfelf, that's one way: the other is, that fhe coming at laft to love him, with as violent a paffion as he lov'd her, fhe kills herfelf. Now my queftion is, which of thefe two perfons fhould fuffer upon this occafion?

Johnf. By my troth, it is a very hard cafe to decide.

Bayes. The hardeft in the world, I'gad, and has puzzled this pate very much. What fay you Mr. Smith?

Smi. Why truly, Mr. Bayes, if it might ftand with your juftice now, I would fpare 'em both.

Bayes. I'gad, and I think---ha---why then I'll make

make him hinder her from killing herfelf. Ay, it
fhall be fo: come, come, bring in the funeral.

Enter a funeral, with the two Ufurpers and Atten-
dants.

Lay it down there, no, no, here Sir: fo now
fpeak.

 K. Ufh. Set down the funeral pile, and let our
   grief
   Receive from its embraces fome relief.
 K. Phyf. Was't not unjuft to ravifh hence her
   breath,
   And in life's ftead, to leave us nought
   but death?
   The world difcovers now its emptinefs,
   And by her lofs demonftrates we have lefs.
 Bayes. Is not this good language now? Is not
that elevated? 'Tis my *non ultra,* I'gad. You muft
know they were both in love with her.
 Smi. With her; with whom?
 Bayes. Why, this is Lardella's funeral.
 Smi. Lardella! Ay, who is fhe?
 Bayes. Why, Sir, the fifter of Drawcanfir. *A

 * *A lady that was drowned at fea,* &c.]
 " On feas I bore thee, and on feas I dy'd,

       " I dy'd:

lady that was drown'd at fea, and had a wave for
her winding-fheet.

K. Ufh. Lardella, O Lardella! from above
   Behold the tragic iffues of our love.
   Pity us finking under grief and pain,
   For thy being caft away upon the main.

Bayes. Look you, now, you fee I told you true.

Smi. Ay, Sir, and I thank you for it, very
kindly.

Bayes. Ay, I'gad, but you will not have patience; honeft Mr.---a---you will not have patience.

Johnf. Pray, Mr. Bayes, who is that Drawcanfir.

Bayes. Why, Sir, a fierce hero, that frights his
miftrefs, fnubbs up kings, baffles armies, and does
what he will, without regard to numbers, good
manners, or juftice.

Johnf. A very pretty character.

Smi. But, Mr. Bayes, I thought your heroes
had ever been men of great humanity and juftice.

Bayes. Yes, they have been fo; but, for my
part, I prefer that one quality of fingly beating

" I dy'd: and for a winding fheet, a wave
" I had; and all the ocean for my grave."
     Conqueft of Granada, part. II. p. 113.

of whole armies, above all your moral virtues put together, I'gad. You fhall fee him come in prefently. Zookers, why don't you read the paper?

[*To the players.*

K. Phyf. O, cry you mercy!

Bayes. Pifh! Nay, you are fuch a fumbler. Come, I'll read it myfelf.

[*Takes a paper from off the coffin.*
Stay, its an ill hand, I muft ufe my fpectacles. This, now, is a copy of verfes, which I make Lardella compofe juft as fhe is dying, with a defign to have it pin'd upon her coffin, and fo read by one of the ufurpers, who is her coufin.

Smi. A very fhrewd defign that, upon my word, Mr. Bayes.

Bayes. And what do you think, now, I fancy her to make love like here in the paper?

Smi. Like a woman, what fhould fhe make love like?

Bayes. O' my word, you are out though, Sir, I'gad you are!

Smi. What then, like a man?

Bayes. No, Sir, like a humble-bee.

Smi. I confefs, that I fhould not have fancy'd.

Bayes. It may be fo, Sir; but it is tho', in order

to

to conform to the opinion of fome of your ancient philofophers, who held the tranfmigration of the foul.

Smi. Very fine.

Bayes. I'll read the title. *To my dear couz. King Phyf.*

Smi. That's a little too familiar with a king, tho', Sir, by your favour, for a humble-bee.

Bayes. Mr. Smith, in other things, I grant your knowledge may be above me; but, as for poetry, give me leave to fay, I underftand that better; it has been longer my practice; it has indeed, Sir. Pray mark it.   [*Reads.*

* Since death my earthly part will thus remove,
I'll come a humble-bee to your chafte love.

---

* *Since death,* &c.] In ridicule of thefe lines.
" ---------------My earthly part,
" Which is my tyrant's right, death will remove,
" I'll come, all foul and fpirit, to your love:
" With filent fteps I'll follow you all day;
" Or elfe before you in the fun-beams play.
" I'll lead you thence to melancholy groves,
" And there repeat the fcenes of our paft loves.
" At night, I will within your curtains peep;
" With empty arms, embrace you, while you fleep:

" In

With filent wings I'll follow you, dear couz;
Or elfe before you in the fun-beams buz.
And when to melancholy groves you come
An airy ghoft, you'll know me by my hum;
For found, being air, a ghoft does well become.

Smi. (*after a paufe*) Admirable!

Bayes. At night into your bofom I will creep,
    And buz but foftly, if you chance to fleep;
    Yet in your dreams I will pafs fweeping by,
    And then both hum and buz before your
        eye;

Johnf. By my troth that's a very great promife.

Smi. Yes, and a moft extraordinary comfort to
boot.

Bayes. Your bed of love from dangers I will
        free;
    But moft from love of any future bee.

" In gentle dreams I often will be by,
" And fweep along before your clofing eye;
" All dangers from your bed I will remove,
" But guard it moft from any future love.
" And when at laft in pity you will die,
" I'll watch your birth of immortality:
" Then, turtle-like, I'll to my mate repair,
" And teach you your firft flight in open air."

Tyrannick Love, p. 25.

And

And when with pity your heart-ftrings fhall
   crack,
With empty arms I'll bear you on my back.
Smi. A pick-a-pack, a pick-a-pack.
Bayes. Ay, I'gad, but is not that *tuant* now, ha ?
Is it not *tuant?* Here's the end.
Then at your birth of immortality,
Like any winged archer, hence I'll fly,
And teach you your firft flutt'ring in the fky.

Johnf. O rare ! This is the moft natural, refin'd
fancy that ever I heard of, I'll fwear.

Bayes. Yes, I think for a dead perfon, it is a
good enough way of making love : For being di-
vefted of her terreftrial part, and all that, fhe is
only capable of thefe little, pretty, amorous de-
figns that are innocent, and yet paffionate. Come,
draw your fwords.

K. Phyf. Come, fword, come fheath thyfelf
     within this breaft,
      Which only in Lardella's tomb can
      reft.

K. Ufh. Come dagger, come, and penetrate
     this heart,
      Which cannot from Lardella's love de-
      part.

        G 3   *Enter*

Enter Pallas.

Pal. Hold, ſtop your murdering hands,
　　At Pallas's commands;
　　For the ſuppoſed dead, O kings,
　　Forbear to act ſuch deadly things.
　　Lardella lives, I did but try
　　If princes for their loves could die,
　　Such celeſtial conſtancy
　　Shall by the Gods rewarded be:
　　And from theſe funeral obſequies
　　A nuptial banquet ſhall ariſe.
　　　[*The coffin opens, and a banquet is diſcover'd.*

Bayes. So, take away the coffin. Now its out:
This is the very funeral of the fair perſon which
Volſcius ſent word was dead; and Pallas, you ſee,
has turn'd it into a banquet.

Smi. Well, but where is the banquet?

Bayes. Nay, look you, Sir, we muſt firſt have
a dance, for joy that Lardella is not dead. Pray,
Sir, give me leave to bring in my things properly
at leaſt.

Smi. That indeed I had forgot: I aſk your pardon.

Bayes. O, d'ye ſo, Sir? I am glad you will
confeſs yourſelf once in an error, Mr. Smith.

　　　　　　　　　　　　　　　　　Dance.

Dance.

K. Uſh. Reſplendent Pallas, we in thee do find
      The fierceſt beauty, and a fiercer mind:
      And ſince to thee Lardella's life we owe,
      We'll ſupple ſtatues in thy temple grow.
K. Phyſ. Well, ſince alive Lardella's found,
      Let in full bowls her health go round.
[*The two Uſurpers take each of them a bowl in their*
                hands.
K. Uſh. But where's the wine.
Pal. That ſhall be mine.
     *Lo, from this conqu'ring lance,
     Does flow the pureſt wine of France.
         [*Fills the bowls out of her lance.*
     And, to appeaſe your hunger, I
     Have in my helmet brought a pye:
     Laſtly, to bear a part with theſe,
     Behold a buckler made of cheeſe.
               [*Vaniſh* Pallas.

---

  * *Lo from this conqu'ring lance,* &c.] See the ſcene of
The Villain, p. 47, &c. where the hoſt furniſhes his gueſts
with a collation out of his cloaths; a capon from his hel-
met, a tanſey out of the lining of his cap, cream out of
his ſcabbard, &c.

          G 4   *Bayes.*

Bayes. There's the banquet. Are you fatisfy'd now, Sir,

Johnf. By my troth, now, that is new, and more than I expected.

Bayes. Yes, I knew this would pleafe you: For the chief art in poetry is to elevate your expectation, and then bring you off fome extraordinary way, ·

Enter Drawcanfir.

K. Phyf. What man is this, that dares difturb our feaft?

Draw. *He that dares drink, and for that
   drink dares die,
  And knowing this, dares yet drink on,
  am I.

Johnf. That is, Mr. Bayes, as much as to fay, that, tho' he would rather die than not drink, yet he would fain drink for all that too.

Bayes. Right; that's the conceit on't.

---

* *What man is that,* &c.] In imitation of
 " *Almab.* Who dares to interrupt my private walk?
 " *Alman.* He who dares love, and for that love muft
  die,
 " And, knowing this, dares yet love on, am I.
      Granada, part. II. p. 115.
        Johnf.

Johns. 'Tis a marvellous good one, I swear.

Bayes. *Now, there are some criticks that have advised me to put out the second *Dare*, and print *Must* in the place on't; but, I'gad, I think 'tis better thus a great deal.

Johns. Whoo! a thousand times!

Bayes. Go on then.

K. Ush. Sir, if you please, we should be glad to know,

How long you here will stay, how soon you'll go?

Bayes. Is not that now, like a well-bred person, I'gad? So modest, so gent!

Smi. O, very like:

Draw. †You shall not know how long I here will stay,

But you shall know I'll take your bowls away.

[*Snatches the bowls out of the king's hands, and drinks 'em off.*

* *Now there are some criticks, &c.*] The passage last cited from the conquest of Granada, was at first wrote,

" He who dares love, and for that love *dares* die,"

but was afterwards amended to *must* die.

† *You shall not know, &c.*] In imitation of,

" *Alman.* I would not now, if thou would'st beg me, stay;

" But I will take my Almahide away."

[*Smi.*

Smi. But, Mr. Bayes, is that, too, modeſt and gent?

Bayes. No, I'gad, Sir; but 'tis great.

K. Uſh. Tho', brother, this grum ſtranger be a
    clown,

He'll leave us ſure a little to gulp
    down.

Draw. *Whoe'er to gulp one drop of this dares
    think,

I'll ſtare away his very power to drink.

[*The two King's ſneak off the ſtage with their attendants.*

†I drink, I huff, I ſtrut, look big, and
    ſtare,

And all this I can do, becauſe I dare.

              [*Exit.*

* *Whoe'er to gulp,* &c.] In ridicule of this,
" *Alman.* Thou dar'ſt not marry her, while I'm in ſight;
" With a bent brow, thy prieſt, and thee, I'll fright:
" And, in that ſcene, which ſhould thy hopes content,
" The thoughts of me ſhall make thee impotent."

           Granada, p. 32.

† *I drink, I huff,* &c.]
" Spite of myſelf, I'll ſtay, fight, love, deſpair:
" And all this I can do, becauſe I dare."

        Granada, part II. p. 89.

           Smi.

Smi. I suppose, Mr. Bayes, this is the fierce hero you spoke of?

Bayes. Yes, but this is nothing: You shall see him, in the last act, win above a dozen battles, one after another, I'gad, as fast as they can possibly come upon the stage.

Johns. That will be a fight worth the seeing indeed.

Smi. But, pray, Mr. Bayes, why do you make the kings let him use 'em so scurvily?

Bayes. Phoo! That is to raise the character of Drawcansir.

Johns. O' my word, that was well thought on.

Bayes. Now, Sirs, I'll shew you a scene indeed, or rather, indeed, the scene of scenes: 'Tis an heroic scene.

Smi. And, pray, Sir, what's your design in this scene?

Bayes. Why, Sir, my design is guilded truncheons, forc'd conceit, smooth verse, and a rant: In fine, if this scene do not take, I'gad, I'll write no more. Come, come in Mr.---a---nay, come in as many as you can. Gentlemen, I must desire you to remove a little, for I must fill the stage.

Smi. Why, fill the stage?

Bayes.

Bayes. O, Sir, becaufe your heroic verfe never founds well, but when the ftage is full.

SCENE II.

Enter Prince Pretty-man *and* Prince Volfcius.

Bayes. Nay, hold, hold; pray, by your leave a little. Look you, Sir, the drift of this fcene is fomewhat more than ordinary: for I make 'em both fall out, becaufe they are not in love with the fame woman.

Smi. Not in love? you mean, I fuppofe, becaufe they are in love, Mr. Bayes.

Bayes. No, Sir, I fay not in love; there's a new conceit for you. Now fpeak.

Pret. Since fate, prince Volfcius, now has fouhd
　　　the way,
　　　For our fo long'd-for meeting here this day,
　　　Lend thy attention to my grand concern.
Volf. I gladly would that ftory from thee learn;
　　　But thou to love doft Pretty-man incline,
　　　Yet love in thy breaft, is not love in mine.
Bayes. Antithefis. Thine and mine.
Pret. Since love itfelf's the fame, why fhould
　　　it be
　　　Diff'ring in you from what it is in me?
　　　　　　　　　　　　　　Bayes.

Bayes. Reafon! I'gad, I love reafoning in verfe.

Volf. Love takes, Camelion-like, a various dye,
 From every plant on which itfelf does lye.

Bayes. Simile!

Pret. Let not thy love the courfe of nature fright,
 Nature does moft in harmony delight.

Volf. How weak a deity would nature prove,
 Contending with the pow'rful god of love?

Bayes. There's a great verfe!

Volf. If incenfe thou will offer at the fhrine,
 Of mighty love, burn it to none but mine.
 Her rofy lips eternal fweets exhale;
 And her bright flame makes all flames elfe
 look pale.

Bayes. I'gad, that is right.

Pret. Perhaps dull incenfe may thy love fuffice;
 But mine muft be ador'd with facrifice.
 All hearts turn afhes, which her eyes con-
 troul,
 The body they confume as well as foul.

Volf. My love has yet a power more divine;
 Victims her altars burn not, but refine:
 Amidft the flames they ne'er give up the
 ghoft;
 But with her looks, revive ftill as they
 roaft.   In

In fpite of pain and death, they're kept
    alive,
Her fiery eyes make 'em in fire furvive.

Bayes. That is as well, I'gad, as I can do,

Volf. Let my Parthenope at length prevail.

Bayes. Civil, I'gad.

Pret. I'll fooner have a paffion for a whale:
    In whofe vaft bulk, tho' ftore of oil doth
        lie,
    We find more fhape, more beauty in a fly.

Smi. That's uncivil, I'gad.

Bayes. Yes, but as far a fetch'd fancy tho', I'gad,
as e'er you faw.

Volf. Soft, Prettyman, let not thy vain pretence
    Of perfect love, defame love's excel-
        lence.
    Parthenope is fure as far above
    All other loves, as above all is love.

Bayes. Ah! I'gad, that ftrikes me.

Pret. To blame my Cloris, gods would not
    pretend.

Bayes. Now mark.

Volf. Were all gods join'd, they could not hope
    to mend

My

My better choice; for fair Parthenope,.
*Gods would, themfelves, ungod them-
felves to fee.

Bayes. Now the rant's a-coming.

Pret. † Durft any of the gods be fo uncivil,
I'd make that god fubfcribe himfelf a
devil.

Bayes. Ay, gadzookers, that's well writ!
[*Scratching his head, his peruke falls off.*

Volf. Couldft thou that god from heaven to
earth tranflate,
He could not fear to want a heav'nly
ftate;
Parthenope on earth can heav'n create. }

---

* *Gods would, themfelves, ungod themfelves to fee.*]
" *Max.* Thou lyeft. There's not a god inhabits there,
" But, for this chriftian, would all heaven forfwear:
" Ev'n Jove would try new fhapes her love to win,
" And in new birds, and unknown beafts would fin; }
" At leaft, if Jove cou'd love like Maximin."
Tyrannick Love, p. 17.

† *Durft any of the gods,* &c.]
" Some god now, if he dare relate what paft,
" Say but he's dead, that god fhall mortal be."
Ibid. p. 7.
" Provoke

Pret. Cloris does heaven itfelf fo far excell,

      She can tranfcend the joys of heav'n in
      hell.

Bayes. There's a bold flight for you `now: S'death I have loft my peruke. Well, gentlemen, this is what I never yet faw any one could write but myfelf. Here's true fpirit and flame all through, I'gad. So, fo, pray clear the ftage.

                 [*He puts 'em off the ftage.*

Johnf. I wonder how the coxcomb has got the knack of writing fmooth verfe thus.

Smi. Why, there's no need of brain for this: 'Tis but fcanning the labours on the finger; but where's the fenfe of it?

Johnf. O, for that he defires to be excufed: *he is too proud a man to creep fervily after fenfe,

    " Provoke my rage no farther, left I be
    " Reveng'd at once upon the gods, and thee."

                   Tyrannick Love, p. 8.
    " What had the gods to do with me or mine?" *Ib.* p. 57.
    * *He is too proud a man*, &c.] Alluding to the follow-ing paffage in the prologue to *Tyrannick Love.*

    " Poets, like lovers, fhould be bold and dare;
    " They fpoil their bufinefs with an over-care;
    " And he, who fervily creeps after fenfe,
    " Is fafe; but ne'er can reach to excellence."

      2   I affure

I affure you. But pray, Mr. Bayes, why is this fcene all in verfe?

Bayes. O, Sir, the fubject is too great for profe.

Smi. Well faid, i'faith, I'll give thee a pot of ale for that anfwer; 'tis well worth it.

Bayes. Come, with all my heart.

" I'll make that god fubfcribe himfelf a devil." That fingle line, I'gad, is worth all that my brother poets ever writ.

Let down the curtain. [*Exeunt.*

END OF THE FOURTH ACT.

ACT V. SCENE I.

Bayes, *and the two gentlemen,*

Bayes. NOW, Gentlemen, I will be bold to fay, I'll fhew you the greateft fcene that ever England faw: I mean not for words, for thofe I don't value; but for ftate, fhew, and magnificence. In fine, I'll juftify it to be as grand to the eye, every whit, I'gad, as that great fcene in Harry-VIII.

and grander too, I'gad; for inſtead of two biſhops, I bring in here four cardinals.

> *The curtain is drawn up, the two uſurping Kings appear in ſtate, with the four Cardinals, Prince Pretty-man, Prince Volſcius, Amarylis, Cloris, Parthenope, &c. before them heralds, and Ser- jeants at arms, with maces.*

Smi. Mr. Bayes, pray what is the reaſon that two of the cardinals are in hats, and the other in caps?

Bayes. Why, Sir, becauſe-----By gad, I won't tell you. Your country-friend, Sir, grows ſo trou-bleſome------

K. Uſh. Now, Sir, to the buſineſs of the day.

K. Phyſ. Speak Volſcius.

Volſ. Dread ſovereign lords, my zeal to you muſt not invade my duty to your ſon; let me in-treat that great prince Pretty-man firſt do ſpeak; whoſe high pre-eminence, in all things do bear the name of good, may juſtly claim that privilege.

Bayes. Here it begins to unfold; you may per-ceive, now, that he is his ſon.

Johnſ. Yes, Sir, and we are very much beholden to you for that diſcovery.

Pret.

Pret. Royal father, upon my knees I beg,

That the illuſtrious Volſcius firſt be heard.

Volſ. That preference is only due to Amaryllis, Sir.

Bayes. I'll make her ſpeak very well, by and by, you ſhall ſee.

Ama. Invincible ſovereigns----   [*Soft muſick.*

K. Uſh. * But ſtay, what ſound is this invades our ears?

K. Phyſ. Sure 'tis the muſick of the moving ſpheres.

Pret. Behold with wonder; yonder comes from far

A god-like cloud, and a triumphant car:

In which our two right kings ſit one by one,

With virgins veſts, and laurel garlands on.

K. Uſh. Then brother Phys, 'tis time we ſhould be gone.

[*The two Uſurpers ſteal out of the throne, and go away.*

• *K. But ſtay, what ſound is this invades our ears ?*]

    " What various noiſes do my ears invade ;

    " And have a concert of confuſion made?"

                              Siege of Rhodes, p. 4.

                    H 3   *Bayes.*

Bayes. Look you now, did not I tell you, that this would be as eafy a change as the other?

Smi. Yes faith you did fo, tho' I confefs, I could not believe you; but you have brought it about I fee.

> [*The two right kings of* Brentford *defcend in the clouds, finging, in white garments; and three fiddlers fitting before them in green.*

Bayes. Now becaufe the two right kings defcend from above, I make 'em fing to the tune and ftile of our modern fpirits.

1 *King.* *Hafte brother king, we are fent from above,

2 *King.* Let us move, let us move;
　　　Move, to remove the fate
　　　Of Brentford's long united ftate.

1 *King.* Tarra, tan, tarra, full eaft and by fouth,

2 *King.* We fail with thunder in our mouth.

---

* *Hafte brother king,* &c.
" *Naker.* Hark, my Damilcar, we are call'd below:
" *Daniel.* Let us go, let us go;
　　" Go, to remove the care
　　" Of longing lovers in defpair, &c."
　　　　　　　　Tyrannick Love, p. 26.

In fcorching noon-day, whilft the tra-
 veller ftays,
Bufy, bufy, bufy, bufy, we buftle along.
Mounted upon warm Phæbus his rays,
 Through the heavenly throng,
  Hafting to thofe
Who will feaft us at night, with a pig's
 petty toes.

1 *King.* And we'll fall with our plate
 In an Olio of hate.

2 *King.* But now fupper's done, the fervitors try,
 Like foldiers, to ftorm a whole half
 moon-pye,

1 *King.* They gather, they gather hot cuftards
 in fpoons,
But, alas, I muft leave thefe half moons,
And repair to my trufty dragoons.

2 *King.* O ftay, for you need not as yet go a-
 ftray,
The tide, like a friend, has brought
 fhips in our way ;
And on their high ropes we will play:
Like maggots in filberds, we'll fnug in
 our fhell,
We'll frifk in our fhell,

We'll

We'll frisk in our shell.

And farewel.

1 *King.* But the ladies have all inclination to
dance,

And the green frogs croak out a coranto
of France.

Bayes. Is not that pretty now? The fiddlers are
all in green.

Smi. Ay, but they play no coranto.

Johns. No, but they play a tune that's a great
deal better.

Bayes. No coranto, quotha! That's a good one,
with all my heart.   Come sing on.

2 *King.*   Now mortals that hear,

How we tilt and career,

With wonder will fear

Th' event of such things as shall never
appear.

1 *King.* Stay you to fulfil what the gods have
decreed,

2 *King.* Then call me to help you, if there shall
be need.

1 *King.* So firmly resolv'd is a true Brentford
king,

To save the distressed, and help to 'em
bring ;

That

That e're a full pot of good ale you can
   swallow,
He's here with a whoop, and gone with
   a hallo.

[Bayes *fillips his finger, and sings after 'em.*

Bayes. He's here with a whoop, and gone with
a hallo. *This, Sir, you muſt know, I thought
once to have brought in with a conjurer.

Johnſ. Ay, that would have been better.

Bayes. No faith, not when you conſider it: for
thus it is more compendious, and does the thing
every whit as well.

Smi. Thing! what thing?

Bayes. Why, bring 'em down again into the
throne, Sir; what thing would you have?

Smi. Well, but methinks the ſenſe of this ſong
is not very plain.

Bayes. Plain! Why, did you ever hear people
in the clouds ſpeak plain? they muſt be all for
flight of fancy, at its full range, without the leaſt
check or controul upon it. When once you tie

* *This, Sir, you muſt know, I thought once to have*
brought in with a conjurer.] See ſuch a contrivance in
Tyrannick Love, act iv. ſcene 1.

up

up fpirits and people in clouds to fpeak plain, you fpoil all.

Smi. Blefs me, what a monfter's this!

[*The two* Kings *'light out of the clouds, and ftep into the throne.*

1 *King.* Come, now to ferious counfel we'll advance,

2 *King.* I do agree, but firft let's have a dance.

Bayes. Right: you did that very well Mr. Cartwright: but firft, let's have a dance. Pray remember that; be fure you do it always juft fo: for it muft be done as if it were the effect of thought, and premeditation. But firft let's have a dance. Pray remember that.

Smi. Well, I can no longer, I muft gag this rogue; there's no enduring of him.

Johnf. No, pr'ythee make ufe of thy patience a little longer: let's fee the end of him now.

[*Dance a grand dance.*

Bayes. This now is an ancient dance, of right belonging to the kings of Brentford; but fince deriv'd, with a little alteration, to the inns of court.

An Alarm. Enter two Heralds.

1 *King.* What faucy groom molefts our privacies?

1 *Her.*

1 *Her.* The army's at the door, and in difguife,
Defires a word with both your majefties.

2 *Her.* Having from Knights-bridge hither
march'd by ftealth,

2 *King.* Bid 'em attend a while and drink our
health.

Smi. How, Mr. Bayes? the army in difguife?

Bayes. Ay, Sir, for fear the ufurpers might difcover them that went out but juft now.

Smi. Why, what if they had difcover'd them?

Bayes. Why, then they had broke the defign.

1 *King.* Here, take five guineas for thofe warlike men.

2 *King.* And here's five more; that makes the
fum juft ten.

1 *Her.* We have not feen fo much, the lord
knows when.   [*Exeunt Heralds.*

1 *King.* Speak on, brave Amaryllis.

Ama. Invincible fovereigns, blame not my modefty,

If at this grand conjuncture-----

[*Drums beat behind the ftage.*

1 *King.* *What dreadful noife is this that comes
and goes?

* 1 *King. What dreadful noife is this,* &c.]

What

Enter a Soldier *with his sword drawn.*

Sold. Haste hence, great Sirs, your royal persons
    save,
For the event of war no mortal knows:
The army, wrangling for the gold you gave,
First fell to words, and then to handy blows.
                         [*Exit.*

Bayes. Is not that now a pretty kind of a stanza,
and a handsome come off?

  2 *King.* O dangerous estate of sovereign power,
      Obnoxious to the change of every hour!

  1 *King.* Let us for shelter in our cab'net stay:
      Perhaps these threat'ning storms may pass
        away.   [*Exeunt.*

Johns. But, Mr. Bayes, did not you promise us
just now to make Amaryllis speak very well.

Bayes. Ay, and so she would have done, but
that they hinder'd her.

Smi. How, Sir, whether you would or no?

What new misfortunes do these cries presage?
  1 *Mess.* Haste all you can, their fury to asswage:
You are not safe from their rebellious rage.
  2 *Mess.* This minute, if you grant not their desire,
They'll seize your person, and your palace fire.
              Grenada, part II. p. 71.
                    Bayes.

Bayes. Ay, Sir, the plot lay fo, that, I vow to gad, it was not to be avoided.

Smi. Marry, that was hard.

Johnf. But pray, who hinder'd her?

Bayes. Why the battle, Sir; that's juft coming in at the door: and I'll tell you now a ftrange thing, tho' I don't pretend to do more than other men, I'gad I'll give you both a whole week to guefs how I'll reprefent this battle.

Smi. I had rather be bound to fight your battle, I affure you, Sir.

Bayes. Whoo! there's it now: fight a battle, there's the common error. I knew prefently where I fhould have you. Why, pray Sir, do but tell me this one thing, can you think it a decent thing, in a battle before ladies, to have men run their fwords through one another, and all that?

Johnf. No faith, 'tis not civil.

Bayes. Right on the other fide, to have a long relation of fquadrons here, and fquadrons there: what is it but dull prolixity?

Johnf. Excellently reafon'd by my troth.

Bayes. Wherefore, Sir, to avoid both thofe in-decorums, * I fum up my whole battle in the re-

* *I fum up my whole battle, &c.*] There needs nothing
more

prefentation of two perfons only, no more: and yet fo lively, that I vow to gad, you would fwear ten thoufand men were at it really engag'd. Do you mark me?

Smi. Yes, Sir; but I think I fhould hardly fwear tho' for all that.

Bayes. By my troth, Sir, but you would tho' when you fee it: for I make 'em both come in, in armour *cap-a-pee*, with their fwords drawn, and hung with a fcarlet ribbon at their wrift, which you know, reprefents fighting enough.

Johnf. Ay, ay, fo much, that if I were in your place, I would make 'em go out again without fpeaking one word.

Bayes. No, there you are out; for I make each of 'em hold a lute in his hand.

Smi. How, Sir? inftead of a buckler?

Bayes. O lord, O lord! inftead of a buckler? Pray, Sir, do you afk no more queftions. I make 'em, Sir, play the battle in *recitativo*. And here's the conceit. Juft at the very fame inftant that

more to explain the meaning of this battle, than the perufal of the firft part of the Siege of Rhodes, which was perform'd in recitative mufick, by feven perfons only: and the paffage out of the *Play-boufe to be let*.

one

one fings, the other, Sir, recovers you his fword, and puts himfelf in a warlike pofture: fo that you have at once your ear entertain'd with mufick and good language; and your eye fatisfied with the garb and accoutrements of war.

Smi. I confefs, Sir, you ftupify me.

Bayes. You fhall fee.

Johnf. But, Mr. Bayes, might not we have a little fighting? for I love thofe plays where they cut and flafh one another upon the ftage, for a whole hour together.

Bayes. Why then, to tell you true, I have con-triv'd it both ways. But you fhall have my *recitativo* firft.

Johnf. Ay, now you are right: there is nothing then can be objected againft it.

Bayes. True, and fo, I'gad, * I'll make it; too, a tragedy in a trice.

> *Enter at feveral docrs, the general and lieu-tenant-general, arm'd cap-a-pee, with each of them a lute in his hand, and his fword*

* *I'll make it, too, a tragedy in a trice.*] Algaura, and the Veftal Virgin are fo contriv'd, by a little alteration towards the latter end of them, that they have been acted both ways, either as tragedies or comedies.

drawn,

drawn, and hung with a scarlet ribbon at his wrist.

Lieut. Gen. Villain, thou lyest.

Gen. * Arm, arm, Gonsalvo, arm ; what ho ?
The lye no flesh can brook I trow.

Lieut. Gen. Advance from Acton, with the musqueteers.

Gen. †Draw down the Chelsey curassiers.

* *Arm, arm, Gonsalvo, arm.*] The Siege of Rhodes begins thus.

" *Admiral.* Arm, arm, Valerius, arm."

† Gen. *Draw down the Chelsey curassiers.*] The third entry in the Siege of Rhodes is thus.

" *Solym.* Pyrrhus, draw down our army wide ;
" Then, from the grofs, two strong reserves divide,
  " And spread the wings,
  " As if we were to fight,
  " In the lost Rhodians fight,
  " With all the western kings :
  " Each with Janizaries line ;
  " The right, and left to Haly's fons affign ?
  " The grofs, to Zangiban.
  " The main artillery
  " To Muftapha shall be :
  " Bring thou the rear, we lead the van."

Lieut.

Lieut. Gen. The band you boaft of Chelfey
    curaffiers

    * Shall, in my Putney pikes, now meet
       their peers.

Gen. Chefwickians, aged and renown'd in fight,
Join with the Hammerfmith brigade.

Lieut. Gen. You'll find my Mortlake boys will
    do them right,
Unlefs by Fulham numbers over-laid.

Gen. Let the left-wing of Twick'nam foot ad-
    vance.

    And line that eaftern hedge.

Lieut. Gen. The horfe I rais'd in Petty-France,
    Shall try their chance,
    And fcour the meadows overgrown with
    fedge.

Gen. Stand, give the word.

Lieut. Gen. Bright fword.

Gen. That may be thine,
    But 'tis not mine.

---

* *Shall, in my Putney pikes, &c.*]
    " More pikes! more pikes! to reinforce
    " That fquadron, and repulfe the horfe."
                   Play-houfe to be let, p. 72.

                          Lieut.

Lieut. Gen. *Give fire, give fire, at once give
     fire,
    And let thefe recreat troops perceive mine
     ire.

Gen. Purfue, purfue ; they fly,
    That firft did give the lye.   [*Exeunt.*

Bayes. This now is not improper I think, becaufe the fpectators know all thefe towns, and
may eafily conceive them to be within the domi-
nions of the two kings of Brentford.

Johnf. Moft exceeding well defign'd !

Bayes. How do you think I have contriv'd to
give a ftop to this battle ?

Smi. How ?

Bayes. By an eclipfe : which, let me tell you,

  * *Give fire, give fire,* &c.]
  " Point all the cannon, and play faft :
" Their fury is too hot to laft.
" That rampier fhakes ; they fly into the town !
  " *Pyr.* March up with thofe referves, to that redoubt ;
" Faint flaves, the Janizaries reel !
" They bend ! they bend ! and feem to feel
" The terrors of a rout.
  " *Muft.* Old Zanger halts, and reinforcement lacks,
  " *Byr.* March on !
  " *Muft.* Advance thofe pikes, and charge their backs.

                           is

is a kind of fancy that was yet never fo much as thought of but by myfelf, and one perfon more that fhall be namelefs.

Enter Lieutenant General.

Lieut. Gen. What mid-night darknefs does in-
   vade the day,
  And fnatch the victor from his conquer'd
   prey?
  Is the fun weary of this bloody fight,
  And winks upon us with the eye of light?
  'Tis an eclipfe. This was unkind, O moon,
  To clap between me and the fun fo foon.
  Foolifh eclipfe; thou this in vain haft done
  My brighter honour had eclips'd the fun:
  But now behold eclipfes two in one. [*Exit.*

Johnf. This is an admirable reprefentation of a battle as I ever fa:

Bayes. Ay, Sir: but how would you fancy to reprefent an eclipfe?

Smi. Why that's to be fuppofed.

Bayes. Suppos'd! Ay, you are ever at your fuppofe: ha, ha, ha. Why you may as well fuppofe the whole play. No, it muft come in upon the ftage, that's certain; but in fome odd way,

that may delight, amufe, and all that. I have a conceit for't, that I am fure is new, and I believe to the purpofe.

Johnf. How's that?

Bayes. Why, the truth is, I took the firft hint of this out of a dialogue between Phœbus and Aurora in the *Slighted Maid:* which by my troth was very pretty; but I think you'll confefs this is a little better.

Johnf. No doubt on't, Mr. Bayes, a great deal better.

[Bayes *hugs* Johnfon, *then turns to* Smith.

Bayes. Ah, dear rogue! But--a--Sir, you have heard, I fuppofe, that your eclipfe of the moon is nothing elfe, but an interpofition of the earth between the fun and moon; as likewife your eclipfe of the fun is caus'd by an interlocation of the moon betwixt the earth and the fun?

Smi. I have heard fome fuch thing indeed.

Bayes. Well, Sir, then what do I, but make the earth, fun and moon, come out upon the ftage, and dance the hey. Hum; and of neceffity, by the very nature of this dance, the earth muft be fometimes between the fun and the moon; and the moon between the earth and the fun: and there you have both your eclipfes, by demonftration.

Johnf. That muft needs be very fine, truly.

Bayes. Yes, it has fancy in't. And then, Sir, that there may be fomething in't, too, of joke, I bring 'em in all finging, and make the moon fell the earth a-bargain. Come, come out eclipfe, to the tune of Tom Tyler.

Enter Luna.

Luna. Orbis, O Orbis!
Come to me, thou little rogue, Orbis.

Enter the Earth.

Orb. *Who calls Terra firma, pray?
Luna. Luna, that ne'er fhines by day.
Orb. What means Luna in a veil?
Luna. Luna means to fhew her tail.
Bayes. There's the bargain.

* Orb. *Who calls Terra firma,* &c.]
" *Phœb.* Who calls the world's great light?
" *Aur.* Aurora, that abhors the night.
" *Phœb.* Why does Aurora, from her cloud,
        " To droufy Phœbus cry fo loud?"
                        Slighted Maid, p. 80.

Enter

Enter Sol, *to the tune of Robin Hood.*

Sol. Fie, fifter, fie ; thou mak'ft me mufe,

    Derry, derry, down,

      To fee the Orb abufe.

Luna. I hope his anger 'twill not move ;

    Since I fhew'd it out of love.

      Hey down, derry down.

Orb. Where fhall I thy true love know,

    Thou pretty, pretty moon?

Luna. *To-morrow foon, e're it be noon,

    On mount Vefuvio.   [*twice*

Sol. Then I will fhine,

          [*To the tune of* Trenchmore.

Orb. And I will be fine.

Luna. † And I will drink nothing but Lippary
wine.

Omnes. And we, &c.

        [*As they dance the hey,* Bayes *fpeaks.*

Bayes. Now the earth's before the moon ; now
the moon's before the fun ; there's the eclipfe again.

* *On Mount Vefuvio.*]

  " The burning mount Vefuvio.

             Slighted Maid, p. 81.

† Luna. *And I will drink nothing but Lippary wine.*]

" Drink, drink wine, Lippary wine."   *Ibid.* p. 81.

                    Smi.

Smi. He's mighti'y taken with this I fee.

Johnf. Ay, 'tis fo extraordinary, how can he chufe?

Bayes. So now, vanifh eclipfe, and enter t'other battle, and fight. Here now, if I am not mif-taken, you will fee fighting enough.

[*A battle is fought between foot and great hobby-horfes. At laft Drawcanfir comes and kills them all on both fides. All the while the battle is fighting,* Bayes *is telling them when to fhout, and fhouts with them.*

Draw. Others may boaft a fingle man to kill;
 But I the blood of thoufands daily fpill.
 Let petty kings the name of parties know,
 Where'er I come I flay both friend and
  foe.
 The fwifteft horfemen my fwift rage con-
  trouls,
 And from their bodies drives their trem-
  bling fouls.
 If they had wings, and to the gods cou'd
  fly,
 I would purfue and beat them thro' the
  fky;

        And

And make proud Jove, with all his thunder, fee,

This fingle arm more dreadful is than he.

[*Exit.*

Bayes. There's a brave fellow for you now, Sirs.
You may talk of your Hectors and Achilles's, and
I know not who; but I defy all your hiftories, and
your romances too, to fhew me one fuch conqueror
as this Drawcanfir.

Johnf. I fwear I think you may.

Smi. But, Mr. Bayes, how fhall all thefe dead
men go off? For I fee none alive to help 'em.

Bayes. Go off! why, as they came on; upon
their legs: how fhould they go off? Why, do you
think the people here don't know they are not
dead? He is mighty ignorant, poor man: your
friend here is very filly, Mr. Johnfon, I'gad, he
is. Ha, ha, ha. Come, Sir, †I'll fhew you

† *I'll fhew you how they fhall go off,* &c.]
Valeria, daughter of Maximin, having killed herfelf for
the love of Porphyrius, when fhe was to be carried off by
the bearers, ftrikes one of them a box on the ear, and
peaks to him thus,

" Hold ! are you mad, you damn'd confounded dog?

" I am to rife and fpeak the epilogue."

Tyrannick Love.

how they fhall go off. Rife, rife, Sirs, and go about your bufinefs. There's a go-off for you now, Ha, ha, ha. Mr. Ivory, a word; gentlemen, I'll be with you prefently.   [*Exit.*

Johnf. Will you fo ? Then we'll be gone.

Smi. Ay, pr'ythee, let's go, that we may preferve our hearing. One battle more will take mine quite away.   [*Exeunt.*

Enter Bayes *and Players.*

Bayes. Where are the gentlemen ?

1 *Play.* They are gone, Sir.

Bayes. Gone ! S'death ! this laft act is beft of all. I'll go fetch 'em again.   [*Exit.*

1 *Play.* What fhall we do, now he is gone away ?

2 *Play.* Why, fo much the better; then let's go to dinner.

3 *Play.* Stay, here's a foul piece of paper : let's fee what 'tis.

3 *or* 4 *Play.* Ay, ay; come, let's hear it.

                    [*Reads the argument of the fifth act.*

3 *Play.* Cloris at length, being fenfible of prince Pretty-man's paffion, confents to marry him; but, juft as they are going to church, Prince Pretty-

                    I 4   man

man meeting by chance with old Joan, the chand
ler's widow, and remembring it was she that
first brought him acquainted with Cloris; out of
a high point of honour, breaks off his match
with Cloris, and marries old Joan. Upon which
Cloris, in despair, drowns herself; and Prince
Pretty-man discontentedly walks by the river-side.
This will never do; 'tis just like the rest. Come,
let's be gone.   [*Exeunt.*

Most of the Play. Ay, pox on't, let's be gone.

Enter Bayes.

Bayes. A plague on them both for me, they
have made me sweat to run after 'em. A couple
of senseless rascals, that had rather go to dinner
than see this play out, with a pox to 'em. What
comfort has a man to write for such dull rogues?
Come, Mr.----a---Where are you. Come away,
quick, quick.

Enter Stage-Keeper.

Stage. Sir, they are gone to dinner.

Bayes. Yes, I know the gentlemen are gone;
but I ask for the players.

Stage. Why, an't please your worship, Sir,
the players are gone to dinner too.

Bayes

Bayes. How! are the players gone to dinner? 'Tis impoffible: The players gone to dinner! I'gad, if they are, I'll make 'em know what it is to injure a perfon that does them the honour to write for 'em, and all that. A company of proud conceited, humorous, crofs-grain'd perfons, and all that. I'gad I'll make 'em the moft contemptible, defpicable, inconfiderable perfons, and all that, in the whole world, for this trick. I'gad I'll be reveng'd on 'em; I'll fell this play to the other houfe.

Stage. Nay, good Sir, don't take away the book; you'll difappoint the company that comes to fee it acted this afternoon.

Bayes. That's all one. I muft referve this comfort to myfelf, my play and I fhall go together, we will not part indeed, Sir.

Stage. But what will the town fay?

Bayes. The town! why, what care I for the town? I'gad the town has us'd me as fcurvily as the players have done: but I'll be reveng'd on them too; for I'll lampoon them all. And fince they will not admit of my plays, they fhall know what a fatyrift I am. And fo farewel to this ftage, I'gad, for ever.   [*Exit* Bayes.
                                                    Enter

Enter Players.

1 *Play.* Come, then, let's fet up bills for another play.

2 *Play.* Ay, ay; we fhall lofe nothing by this, I warrant you.

1 *Play.* I am of your opinion: but, before we go, let's fee Haynes and Shirley practife the laft dance; for that may ferve us another time.

2 *Play.* I'll call 'em in: I think they are but in the tiring-room.   [*The dance done.*

1 *Play.* Come, come; let's go away to dinner.

E P I.

E P I L O G U E.

THE play is at an end, but where's the plot?
That circumſtance the poet Bayes forgot.
And we can boaſt, tho' 'tis a plotting age,
No place is freer from it than the ſtage.
The ancients plotted tho', and ſtrove to pleaſe,
With ſenſe that might be underſtood with eaſe:
They ev'ry ſcene with ſo much wit did ſtore,
That who brought any in, went out with more.
But this new way of wit does ſo ſurprize,
Men loſe their wits in wondering where it lies.
If it be true that monſtrous births preſage,
The following miſchiefs that afflict the age;
And ſad diſaſters to the ſtate proclaim:
Plays, without head or tail, may do the ſame.
Wherefore for ours, and for the kingdom's peace,
May this prodigious way of writing ceaſe.
Let's have, at leaſt, once in our lives, a time,
When we may hear ſome reaſon, not all rhyme:
We have this ten years felt its influence;
Pray, let this prove a year of proſe and ſenſe.

EPILOGUE.

THE

CHANCES.

A

COMEDY.

PROLOGUE.

OF all men, thofe have reafon leaft to care,
For being laugh'd at, who can laugh their fhare:
And that's a thing our author's apt to ufe,
Upon occafion, when no man can chufe.
Suppofe now, at this inftant, one of you
Were tickled by a fool, what would you do?
'Tis ten to one you'd laugh: here's juft the cafe,
For there are fools that tickle with their face.
Your gay fool tickles with his drefs and motions,
But your grave fool of fools, with filly notions.
Is it not then unjuft that fops fhould ftill
Force one to laugh, and then take laughing ill?
Yet fince perhaps to fome it gives offence,
That men are tickl'd at the want of fenfe;
Our author thinks he takes the readieft way,
To fhew all he has laugh'd at here fair play.
For if ill writing be a folly thought,
Correcting ill is fure a greater fault.
Then gallants laugh, but chufe the right place firft,
For judging ill is, of all faults, the worft.

Dramatis

DRAMATIS PERSONÆ.

Duke of Ferrara.
Petruchio, governor of Bolognia.
Don John,⎫ two Spanish gentlemen and
Don Frederick,⎭ comerades.
Antonio, an old stout gentleman, Kinsman to
    Petruchio.
Three gentlemen, friends to the Duke.
Two gentlemen, friends to Petruchio.
Francisco, a musician, Antonio's boy.
Peter Vecchio, a teacher of Latin and musick, a
    reputed wizard.
Peter and⎫ two servants to Don John and
Anthony,⎭ Frederick.
A Surgeon.

W O M E N.

Constantia, Sister to Petruchio, and Mistress to
    the Duke.
Gentlewoman, Servant to Constantia.
Old gentlewoman, landlady to Don John and
    Frederick.
Constantia, a whore to old Antonio.
Bawd.

THE

THE

CHANCES.

ACT I. SCENE I.

Enter Peter *and* Anthony, *two Servants.*

Pet. WOULD we were removed from this
    town, Anthony.
That we might taſte ſome quiet: for my own part,
I'm almoſt melted with continual trotting
After inquiries, dreams and revelations,
Of who knows whom or where, ſerving wenching
    ſoldiers!
I'll ſerve a prieſt in Lent firſt, and eat bell-ropes.
    Ant. Thou art the forward'ſt fool------
    Pet. Why, good tame Anthony?
Tell me but this; to what end came we hither?
    Ant. To wait upon our maſters.
    Pet. But how, Anthony?
Anſwer me that. Reſolve me there, good Anthony.
    Ant. To ſerve their uſes.
    Pet. Shew your uſes, Anthony.
    Ant. To be employed in any thing.
    Pet. No, Anthony;
Not any thing, I take it; nor that thing

VoL. I.   K   We

We travel to difcover, like new iflands;
A falt itch, ferve fuch ufes! In things of moment,
Concerning things I grant ye, not things errant:
Sweet ladies things, and things to thank the fur-
    geon:
In no fuch things, fweet Anthony; put cafe-----
   Ant. Come, come, all will be mended: this
    invifible woman,
Of infinite report for fhape and beauty,
That bred all this trouble to no purpofe,
They are determin'd now no more to think on.
   Pet. Were there ever
Men known to run mad with report before?
Or wander after what they know not where
To find? or, if found, how to enjoy? Are men's
    brains
Made now a-days of malt, that their affections
Are never fober, but like drunken people
Founder at every new fame? I do believe
That men in love are ever drunk, as drunken men
Are ever loving.
   Ant. Pr'ythee, be thou fober,
And know that they are none of thofe, not guilty
Of the leaft vanity in love, only a doubt
Fame might too far report, or rather flatter
                      The

The graces of this woman, made them curious
To find the truth, which fince they find fo
Lock'd up from their fearches, they are now refolv'd
To give the wonder over.

Pet. Would they were refolv'd
To give me fome new fhoes too : for I'll be fworn
Thefe are e'en worn out to the reafonable foals
In their good worfhips bufinefs : and fome fleep
Would not do much amifs, unlefs they mean
To make a bell-man of me.   Here they come.

[*Exeunt.*

Enter Don John *and* Frederick.

John. I would we could have feen her tho': for
   fure
She muft be fome rare creature, or report lyes,
All men's reports too.

Fred. I could well wifh I had feen Conftantia ;
But, fince fhe is fo conceal'd : plac'd where
No knowledge can come near her ; fo guarded
As 'twere impoffible, tho' known, to reach her,
I have made up my belief.

· *John.* Hang me from this hour,
If I more think upon her ;
But, as fhe came a ftrange report unto me,
So the next fame fhall lofe her.

K 2   *Fred.*

Fred. 'Tis the beſt way ꞉
But whither are you walking ?

John. My old round,
After my meat, and then to bed.

Fred. 'Tis healthful.

John. Will not you ſtir ?

Fred. I have a little buſineſs.

John. I'd lay my life this lady ſtill—...

Fred. Then you would loſe it.

John. Pray let's walk together.

Fred. Now I cannot.

John. I have ſomething to impart.

Fred. An hour hence
I will not miſs to meet you.

John. Where ?

Fred. I' th' high-ſtreet ;
For, not to lye, I have a few devotions
To do firſt, then I am yours.

John. Remember.   [*Exeunt.*

S C E N E   II.

Enter Petruchio, Antonio, *and two gentlemen.*

Ant. Cut his wind-pipe, ſ ſay.

1 *Gent.* Fie, Antonio.

                                        Ant.

Ant. Or knock his brains out firſt, and then
     forgive him.
If you do thruſt, be ſure it be to th' hilts,
A ſurgeon may ſee thro' him.

   1 *Gent.* You are too violent.

   2 *Gent.* Too open, undiſcreet.

   Petr. Am I not ruin'd?
The honour of my houſe crack'd? my blood
     poiſon'd?
My credit and my name?

   2 *Gent.* Be ſure it be ſo,
Before ye uſe this violence. Let not doubt,
And a ſuſpecting anger ſo much ſway you;
Your wiſdom may be queſtion'd.

   Ant. I ſay, kill him,
And then diſpute the cauſe; cut off what may be,
And what is ſhall be ſafe.

   2 *Gent.* Hang up a true man,
Becauſe 'tis poſſible he may be thieviſh;
Alas, is this good ʹuſtice?

   Petr. I know as certain
As day muſt come again; as clear as truth,
And open as belief can lay it to me,
That I am baſely wrong'd, wrong'd above recom-
     pence,

Malicioufly abus'd, blafted for ever,
In name and honour, loft to all remembrance,
But what is fmear'd and fhameful; I muft kill him,
Neceffity compels me.

   1 *Gent.* But think better.

   Petr. There is no other cure left; yet witnefs
      with me
All that is fair in man, all that is noble,
I am not greedy of this life I feek for,
Nor thirft to fhed man's blood; and would 'twere
      poffible,
I wifh it with my foul, fo much I tremble
To offend the facred image of my Maker,
My fword could only kill his crimes; no, 'tis
Honour, honour, my noble friends, that idol ho-
      nour,
That all the world now worfhips, not Petruchio,
Muft do this juftice.

   Ant. Let it once be done,
And 'tis no matter, whether you or honour,
Or both be acceffary.

   2 *Gent.* Do you weigh, Petruchio,
The value of the perfon, power, and greatnefs,
And what this fpark may kindle?

   Petr. To perform it,

                   So

So much I am ty'd to reputation,
And credit of my houfe, let it raife wild fires,
And ftorms that tofs me into everlafting ruin.
Yet I muft through, if ye dare fide me.

   Ant. Dare?

   Petr. Y' are friends indeed, if not.

   2 *Gent.* Here's none flies from you, ·
Do it in what defign you pleafe, we'll back ye.

   1 *Gent.* Is the caufe fo mortal, nothing but
      his life?----

   Petr. Believe me,
A lefs offence has been the defolation
Of a whole name.

   2 *Gent.* No other way to purge it?

   Petr. There is, but never to be hop'd for.

   2 *Gent.* Think an hour more,
And if then you find no fafer road to guide you,
We'll fet our refts too.

   Ant. Mine's up already,
And hang him for my part, goes lefs than life.

   2 *Gent.* If we fee noble caufe, 'tis like our
      fwords
May be as free and forward as your words.

                  [*Exeunt.*

      K 4   SCENE

SCENE III.

Enter Don John.

John. The civil order of this city Naples,
Makes it belov'd and honour'd of all travellers,
As a moſt ſafe retirement in all troubles;
Beſides, the wholſome ſeat and noble temper
Of thoſe minds that inhabit it, ſafely wiſe,
And to all ſtrangers courteous; but I ſee,
My admiration has drawn night upon me,
And longer to expect my friend, may pull me
Into ſuſpicion of too late a ſtirrer,
Which all good governments are jealous of.
I'll home, and think at liberty: yet certain,
'Tis not ſo far night as I thought: for ſee,
A fair houſe yet ſtands open, yet all about it
Are cloſe; and no light's ſtirring; there may be
       foul play;
I'll venture to look in; if there be knaves,
I may do a good office.   [*Woman within.*
  Within. Signior!
  John. What? how is this?
  Within. Signor Fabricio!
  John. I'll go nearer.
  Within. Fabricio!

                                        John.

John. This is a woman's tongue, here may be
    good done.

Within. Who's there? Fabricio?

John. Ay.

Within. Where are you?

John. Here.

Within. O come for heaven's fake!

John. I muft fee what this means.

Enter Woman *with a child.*

Within. I have ftay'd this long hour for you;
    make no noife:

For things are in ftrange trouble here; be fecret,

'Tis worth your care; be gone, now, more eyes
    watch us

Than may be for our fafeties.

John. Hark ye.

Within. Peace, good night.   [*Exit.*

John. She's gone, and I am loaden, fortune for
    me,

It weighs well, and it feels well; it may chance

To be fome pack of worth. By the mafs, 'tis
    heavy;

If it be coin or jewels, it is worth welcome:

I'll ne'er refufe a fortune; I am confident

'Tis

'Tis of no common price : now to my lodging :
If it be right, I'll blefs this night. *[Exit.*

S C E N E IV.

Enter Don Frederick.

Fred. 'Tis ftrange,
I cannot meet him ; fure he has encounter'd
Some light o' love or other, and there means
To play at in and in for this night. Well, Don
    John,
If you do fpring a leak, or get an itch,
Till you claw off your curl'd pate, then your
    night walks----
You muft ftill be a boot-haling ; one round more,
Tho' it be late, I'll venture to difcover you,
I do not like your out-leaps. *[Exit.*

S C E N E V.

Enter Duke, *and three* Gentlemen.

Duke. Welcome to town, are ye all fit ?
1 *Gent.* To point, Sir.
Duke. Where are the horfes ?
2 *Gent.* Where they were appointed.
Duke. Be private, and whatfoever fortune
Offer itfelf, let us ftand fure.

3 *Gent.*

3 *Gent.* Fear us not.

'Ere you fhall be endanger'd, or deluded,

We'll make a black night on't.

Duke. No more, I know it ;

You know your quarters.

  1 *Gent.* Will you go alone, Sir ?

Duke. Ye fhall not be far from me, the leaft
    noife

Shall bring you to my refcue.

  2 *Gent.* We are counfell'd.   [*Exeunt.*

S C E N E   VI.

Enter Don John.

John. Was ever man fo paid for being curious ?

Ever fo bobb'd for fearching out adventures,

As I am ? Did the devil lead me ? Muft I needs
    be peeping

Into men's houfes where I had no bufinefs,

And make myfelf a mifchief ? 'tis well carried ;

I muft take other men's occafions on me,

And be I know not whom : moft finely handled :

What have I got by this now ? what's the pur-
    chafe ?

A piece of evening arras work, a child,

Indeed an infidel : This comes of peeping :

                  A lump

A lump got out of lazinefs; good white bread,
Let's have no bawling with ye: 'Sdeath, have I
Known wenches thus long, all the ways of wenches,
Their fnares and fubtilties? have I read over
All their fchool learning, div'd into their quid-
  dities,
And am I now bum-fiddl'd with a baftard,
Fetch'd over with a card of five, and in my old
  days,
After the dire maffacre of a million
Of maidenheads, caught the common way, 'ith'
  night too,
Under another's name, to make the matter
Carry more weight about it? Well, Don John,
You will be wifer one day, when you've purchas'd
A bevy of thofe butter-prints together,
With fearching out concealed iniquities,
Without commiffion: why, it would never grieve
  me,
If I had got this ginger-bread: never ftirr'd me
So I had a ftroke for't; it had been juftice
Then to have kept it; but to raife a dairy
For other men's adulteries, confume myfelf in
  candles,
And fcouring work, in nurfes, bells, and babies,
         Only

Only for charity, for meer I thank you,
A little troubles me.: the leaſt touch for it,
Had but my breeches got it, it had contented me
Whoſe e'er it is. Sure it had a wealthy mother,
For 'tis well cloath'd, and, if I be not cozen'd,
Well lin'd within : to leave it here were barbarous,
And ten to one would kill it ; a worſe ſin
Than his that got it : well, I will diſpoſe on't,
And keep it, as they keep death's heads in rings,
To cry *momento* to me ; no more peeping :
Now all the danger is, to qualify
The good old gentlewoman, at whcſe houſe we
        live ;
For ſhe will fall upon me with a catechiſm
Of four hours long : I muſt endure all ;
For I will know this mother: come, good wonder,
Let you and I be jogging : your ſtarv'd treble
Will waken the rude watch elſe : all that be
Curious night-walkers, may they find my fee.

                                        [*Exit.*

S C E N E VII.

Enter Frederick.

Fred. Sure he's gone home:
I have beaten all the purlieus,

                    I   But

But cannot bolt him : if he be a-bobbing,
'Tis not my care can cure him ; to-morrow morn-
    ing
I fhall have further knowledge from a furgeon.----
Where he lies moor'd to mend his leaks.

Enter 1 Conftantia.

  Con. I am ready,
And through a world of dangers am flown to you;
Be full of hafte and care, we are undone elfe :
Where are your people ? which way muft we
    travel ?
For heaven's fake ftay not here, Sir.
  Fred. What may this prove ?
  Con. Alas, I am miftaken, loft, undone,
For ever perifh'd : Sir, for heaven's fake tell me,
Are you a gentleman ?
  Fred. I am.
  Con. Of this place ?
  Fred. No, born in Spain.
  Con. As ever you lov'd honour,
As ever your defires may gain their ends,
Do a poor wretched woman but this benefit,
For I am forc'd to truft ye.
  Fred. Y've charm'd me,

                        Huma

Humanity and honour bids me help you;
And if I fail your truft-----
  Con. The time's too dangerous
To ftay your proteftations: I believe you,
Alas! I muft believe you: from this place,
Good noble Sir, remove me inftantly.
And for a time, where nothing but yourfelf,
And honeft converfation may come near me,
In fome fecure place fettle me.   What I am,
And why thus boldly I commit my credit
Into a ftranger's hand, the fears and dangers
That force me to this wild courfe, at more leifure
I fhall reveal unto you.
  Fred. Come be hearty.
He muft ftrike through my life that takes
You from me.   [*Exeunt.*

S C E N E   VIII.

Enter Petruchio, Antonio, *and two* Gentlemen.

  Petr. He will fure come.   Are ye all well arm'd?
  Ant. Never fear us:
Here's that will make 'em dance without a fiddle.
  Petr. We are to look for no weak foes, my
      friends,
Nor unadvifed ones.

                    2   *Ant.*

Ant. The beſt gameſters make the beſt play;
We ſhall fight cloſe and home then.

 1 *Gent.* Antonio,
You are a thought too bloody.

 Ant. Why? all phyſicians
And penny almanacks allow the opening
Of veins this month: Why do ye talk of bloody?
What come we for? to fall to cuffs for apples!
What, would you make the cauſe a cudgel quarrel?

 Petr. Speak ſoftly, gentle couſin.

 Ant. I will ſpeak truly;
What ſhould men do ally'd to theſe diſgraces,
Lick o'er his enemy, ſit down, and dance him?

 2 *Gent.* You are as far o'th' bow hand now.

 Ant. And cry,
That my fine boy, thou wilt do ſo no more child.

 Petr. Here are no ſuch cold pities.

 Ant. By St. Jaques,
They ſhall not find me one! here's old tough
  Andrew,
A ſpecial friend of mine, if he but hold,
I'll ſtrike 'em ſuch a horn-pipe: knocks I come
  for,
And the beſt blood I light on; I profeſs it,

          Not

Not to fcare coftermongers; if I lofe my own,
My audit's loft, and farewel five and fifty.

 Petr. Let's talk no longer, place yourfelves
  with filence,

As I direfted ye; and when time calls us,
As ye are friends, fo fhew yourfelves.

 Ant. So be it;   [*Exeunt.*

S C E N E IX.

Enter Don John *and his* Land-lady.

 Land. Nay, fon, if this be your regard.

 John. Good mother.

 Land. Good me no goods, your coufin and
  yourfelf

Are welcome to me, whilft you bear yourfelves
Like honeft and true gentlemen : bring hither
To my houfe, that have ever been reputed
A gentlewoman of a decent and fair carriage,
And fo behaved myfelf !----

 John. I know you have.

 Land. Bring hither, as I fay, to make my name
Stink in my neighbours noftrils, your devices,
Your brats got out of Allicant, and broken oaths !
Your linfey-wolfey work, your hafty-puddings !
I fofter up your filch'd iniquities !

Vol. I.   L   Y'are

Y'are deceiv'd in me, Sir, I am none
Of thofe receivers.

John. Have I not fworn unto you,
'Tis none of mine, and fhew'd you how I found it?

Land. Ye found an eafy fool, that let you get it.

John. Will you hear me?

Land. Oaths! What care you for oaths to gain
　　your ends,
When ye are high and pamper'd? What faint
　　know ye?
Or what religion, but your purpos'd lewdnefs,
Is to be look'd for of ye? nay, I will tell ye,
You will then fwear like accus'd cut-purfes,
As far off truth too; and lye beyond all falconers:
I'm fick to fee this dealing.

John. Heaven forbid, mother.

Land. Nay, I am very fick.

John. Who waits there?

Pet. Sir? (*within.*)

John. Bring down the bottle of Canary wine.

Land. Exceeding fick, heaven help me.

John. Hafte ye, Sirrah,
I muft e'en make her drunk; nay, gentle mother.

Land. Now fie upon ye, was it for this purpofe
　　　　　　　　　　　　　　　　　　　　You

You fetch'd your evening walks for your devotions,
For this pretended holinefs? no weather,
Not before day, could hold ye from the mattins.
Were thefe your bo-peep prayers? y've pray'd
    well,
And with a learn'd zeal watch'd well too: your
    faint
It feems was pleas'd as well: ftill ficker, ficker!

Enter Peter *with a bottle of wine.*

John. There is no talking to her till I have
    drench'd her.
Give me; here, mother, take a good round draught,
'Twill purge fpleen from your fpirits: deeper,
    mother.
Land. Ay, ay, fon; you imagine this will mend
    all.
John. All, ay faith, mother.
Land. I confefs the wine
Will do his part.
John. I'll pledge ye.
Land. But, fon John.
John. I know your meaning, mother; touch it
    once more.
Alas! you look not well, take a round draught,

It warms the blood well, and reſtores the colour,
And then we'll talk at large.

    Land. A civil gentleman!
A ſtranger! one the town holds a good regard of!

    John. Nay I will ſilence the there.

    Land. One that ſhould weigh his fair name! oh,
        a ſtitch!

    John. There's nothing better for a ſtitch, good
        mother;
Make no ſpare of it; as you love your health,
Mince not the matter.

    Land. As I ſaid, a gentleman,
Lodged in my houſe! now heaven's my comfort,
        Signior!

    John. I look'd for this.

    Land. I did not think you would have us'd me
        thus;
A woman of my credit; one, heaven knows,
That loves you but too tenderly.

    John. Dear mother,
I ever found your kindneſs, and acknowledge it.

    Land. No, no, I am a fool to counſel you.
        Where's the infant?
Come, let's ſee your workmanſhip.

                       John.

John. None of mine, mother;
But there 'tis, and a lufty one.
. *Land.* Heav'n blefs thee,
Thou hadft a hafty making; but the beft is,
'Tis many a good man's fortune: as I live,
Your own eyes, Signior; and the neither lip
As like you, as you had fpit it.
. *John.* I am glad on't.
Land. Blefs, me, what things are thefe?
John. I thought my labour
Was not all loft, 'tis gold, and thefe are jewels,
Both rich, and right I hope.
Land. Well, well, fon John,
I fee ye're a woodman, and can chufe
Your deer, tho' it be i'th' dark, all your difcretion
Is not yet loft; this was well clap'd aboard:
Here I am with ye now, when, as they fay,
Your pleafure comes with profit; when you muft
     needs do;
Do where you may be done to, 'tis a wifdom,
Becomes a young man well: be fure of one thing,
Lofe not your labour and your time together,
It feafons of a fool; fon, time is precious,
Work warily whilft you have it; fince you muft
     traffic

          Sometimes

Sometimes this flippery way, take fure hold, Sig-
    nior,
Trade with no broken merchants, make your
    lading
As you would make your reft, adventuroufly,
But with advantage ever.

    John. All this time, mother,
The child wants looking to, wants meat and nurfes.

    Land. Now bleffing o'thy heart, it fhall have all,
And inftantly; I'll feek a nurfe myfelf, fon:
'Tis a fweet child; ah my young Spaniard!
Take you no further care, Sir.

    John. Yes of thefe jewels,
I muft by your good leave, mother; thefe are yours,
To make your care the ftronger; for the reft
I'll find a mafter: the gold for bringing up on't
I freely render to your charge.

    Land. No more words,
Nor any more children, good fon, as you love me.
This may do well.

    John. I fhall obferve your morals.
But where's Don Frederick, mother?

    Land. Ten to one
About the like adventure; he told me
He was to find you out.   [*Exit.*
                           John.

John. Why fhould he ftay thus?

There may be fome ill chance in't: fleep I will not,

Before I have found him. Now this woman's
    pleas'd,

I'll feek my friend out, and my care is eas'd.

[*Exit.*

S C E N E X.

Enter Duke *and thrée* Gentlemen.

1 *Gent.* Believe, Sir, 'tis as poffible to do it,

As to move the city; the main faction

Swarms through the ftreets like hornets, and with
    angers

Able to ruin ftates, no fafety left us,

Nor means to die like men, if inftantly

You draw not back again.

Duke. May he be drawn

And quarter'd too, that turns now; were I more
    fure

Of death than thou art of thy fears, and of
    deaths

More than thofe fears are too----

1 *Gent.* Sir, I fear not.

L 4

Duke.

Duke. I would not break my vow, ſtart from
    my honour,
Becauſe I may find danger ; wound my ſoul,
To keep my body ſafe.
    1 *Gent.* I ſpeak not, Sir,
Out of a baſeneſs to you.
    Duke. No, nor do not
Out of a baſeneſs leave me : what is danger
More, than the weakneſs of our apprehenſions ?
A poor cold part o'th' blood : who takes it hold of ?
Cowards and wicked livers : valiant minds
Were made the maſters of it, and as hearty ſea-
    men,
In deſperate ſtorms, ſtem with a little rudder
The tumbling ruins of the ocean ;
So with their cauſe and ſwords do they do dangers.
Say we were ſure to die all in this venture,
As I am confident againſt it ; is there any
Amongſt us of ſo fat a ſenſe, ſo pamper'd,
Would chuſe luxuriouſly to lie a-bed,
And purge away his ſpirits ? ſend his ſoul out
In ſugar-ſops, and ſyrups? give me dying
As dying out to be, upon mine enemy,
Parting with mankind, by a man that's manly :
                          Let

Let 'em be all the world, and bring along
Cain's envy with them, I will on.

  2 Gent. You may, Sir,
But with what fafety?

  1 Gent. Since 'tis come to dying,
You fhall perceive, Sir, that here be thofe amongft us
Can die as decently as other men,
And with as little ceremony. On, brave Sir,

  Duke. That's fpoken heartily.

  1 Gent. And he that flinches,
May he die loufy in a ditch.

  Duke. No more dying,
There's no fuch danger in't:
What's a clock?

  3 Gent. Somewhat above your hour.

  Duke. Away then quickly,
Make no noife, and no trouble will attend us.

                       [Exeunt.

SCENE XI.

Enter Frederick *and* Anthony *with a candle.*

  Fred. Give me the candle: fo, go you out that way.

  Ant. What have we now to do?

                       Fred.

Fred. And o'your life, Sirrah,
Let none come near the door without my know-
  ledge,
No, not my landlady, nor my friend.
  Ant. 'Tis done, Sir.
  Fred. Nor any ferious bufinefs that concerns me.
  Ant. Is the wind there again?
  Fred. Be gone.
  Ant. I am, Sir.   [*Exit.*
  Fred. Now enter without fear——

        Enter 1ƒt Conftantia *with a jewel.*

And noble lady,
That fafety and civility you wifh'd for
Shall truly here attend you: No rude tongue,
Nor rough behaviour knows this place? no wifhes,
Beyond the moderation of a man,
Dare enter here: Your own defirès and innocence,
Join'd to my vow'd obedience, fhall protect you.
  Con. You are truly noble,
And worth a woman's truft: Let it become me,
(I do befeech you, Sir) for all your kindnefs,
To render with my thanks this worthlefs trifle;
I may be longer troublefome.
  Fred. Fair offices

                                          Are

Are ftill their own rewards: heaven blefs me, lady,
From felling civil court'fies : May it pleafe ye,
If you will force a favour to oblige me,
Draw but that cloud afide, to fatisfy me
For what good angel I am engag'd.

   Con. It fhall be;
For I am truly confident you are honeft :
The piece is fcarce worth looking on.

   Fred. Truft me,
The abftract of all beauty, foul of fweetnefs!
Defend me, honeft thoughts, I fhall grow wild
    elfe.
What eyes are there, rather what little heavens
To ftir men's contemplations! What a paradife
Runs thro' each part fhe has! Good blood, be
    temperate,
I muft look off: Too excellent an object
Confounds the fenfe that fees it. Noble lady,
If there be any farther fervice to caft on me,
Let it be worth my life, fo much I honour you,
Or the engagement of whole families.

   Con. Your fervice is too liberal, worthy Sir;
Thus far I fhall intreat.——

   Fred. Command me, lady,
You make your power too poor.

                           Con.

Con. That prefently,
With all convenient hafte, you would retire
Unto the ftreet you found me in.

Fred. 'Tis done.

Con. There, if you find a gentleman opprefs'd
With force and violence, do a man's office,
And draw your fword to refcue him.

Fred. He's fafe,
Be what he will, and let his foes be devils,
Arm'd with your beauty, I fhall conjure 'em.
Retire, this key will guide ye: all things neceffary
Are there before ye.

Con. All my prayers go with you.   [*Exit.*

Fred. You clap on proof upon me: Men fay
       gold
Does all, engages all, works through all dangers:
Now, I fay, beauty can do more: The king's ex-
       chequer
Nor all his wealthy Indies, could not draw me
Through half thofe miferies this piece of pleafure
Might make me leap into: we are all like fea-cards,
All our endeavours and our motions,
(As they do to the north) ftill point to beauty,
Still to the faireft: for a handfome woman,
(Setting my foul afide) it fhould go hard,

                                        But

But I would ſtrain my body : Yet to her,
Unleſs it be her own free gratitude,
Hopes ye ſhall die, and thou, tongue, rot within me,
Ere I infringe my faith : now to my reſcue. [*Exit.*

END OF THE FIRST ACT.

ACT II.   SCENE I.

Enter Duke *purſued by* Petruchio, Antonio, *and that faction.*

Duke. YOU will not all oppreſs me ?
  Ant. Kill him i' th' wanton eye : let me come
    to him.
  Duke. Then you ſhall buy me dearly.
  Petr. Say you ſo, Sir ?
  Ant. I ſay, cut his wezond, ſpoil his peeping :
Have at your love-ſick heart, Sir.

Enter Don John.

John. Sure 'tis fighting.
My friend may be engag'd : Fie, gentlemen,
This is unmanly odds.
              [Duke *falls,* Don John *beſtrides him.*
                            Ant. .

Ant. I'll ſtop your mouth, Sir.

John. Nay, then have at thee freely:

There's a plumb, Sir, to ſatisfy your longing.

Petr. Away; I hope I have ſped him: here
　　comes reſcue,

We ſhall be endanger'd: Where's Antonio?

Ant. I muſt have one thruſt more, Sir.

John. Come up to me.

Ant. A miſchief confound your fingers.

Petr. How is it?

Ant. Well.

H'as given me my *quietus eſt*; I felt him

In my ſmall guts; I'm ſure h'as feez'd me;

This comes of ſiding with you.

2 Gent. Can you go, Sir?

Ant. I ſhould go, man, if my head were off,

Never talk of going.

Petr. Come, all ſhall be well then,

I hear more reſcue coming.　　[*Trampling within.*

Enter the Duke's *faƈtion.*

Ant. Let's turn back then:

My ſcull's uncloven yet, let me but kill.

Petr. Away for heaven's ſake with him.　[*Exit.*

John. How is it?

　　I

Duke.

Duke. Well, Sir,
Only a little ftagger'd.

Duke's Faƈt. Let's purfue 'em.

Duke. No, not a man, I charge ye: Thanks,
 good coat,
Thou haft fav'd me a fhrewd welcome: 'twas
 put home too,
With a good mind, I'm fure on't.

John. Are you fafe, then?

Duke. My thanks to you, brave Sir, whofe
 timely valour,
And manly courtefy came to my refcue.

John. You had foul play offer'd you, and fhame
 befal him,
That can pafs by oppreffion.

Duke. May I crave, Sir,
But thus much honour more, to know your name?
And him I am fo bound to?

John. For the bond, Sir,
'Tis every good man's tye: To know me farther
Will little profit ye; I am a ftranger,
My country Spain, my name Don John, a gentleman
That came abroad to travel.

Duke. I have heard, Sir,
Much worthy mention of you, yet I find
Fame fhort of what you are.   *John.*

John. You are pleafed, Sir,
To exprefs your courtefy : May I demand
As freely what you are, and what mifchance
Caft you into this danger?

Duke. For this prefent
I muft defire your pardon : You fhall know me
Ere it be long, Sir, and a nobler thanks,
Than now my will can render.

John. Your will's your own, Sir.

Duke. What is't you look for, Sir? have you
    loft any thing?

John. Only my hat i'th'fcuffle; fure thefe fellows
Were night-fnaps.

Duke. No, believe, Sir; Pray ufe mine,
For 'twill be hard to find your own now.

John. No, Sir,

Duke. Indeed ye fhall, I can command another;
I do befeech you, honour me.

John. Well, Sir, then I will,
And fo I'll take my leave.

Duke. Within thefe few days
I hope I fhall be happy in your knowledge.
Till when I love your memory.   [*Exit cum fuis*

John. I yours.

Enter

Enter Don Frederick.

This is some noble fellow.

Fred. 'Tis his tongue sure.

Don John.

John. Don Frederick.

Fred. Y' are fairly met, Sir.

I thought ye had been a bat-fowling: pr'ythee
    tell me

What revelations hast thou had to-night,

That home was never thought of:

John. Revelations !

I'll tell thee, Frederick: But, before I tell thee,

Settle thy understanding.

Fred. 'Tis prepar'd, Sir.

John. Why, then, mark what shall follow :
    This night, Frederick,

This baudy night----

Fred. I thought no less.

John. This blind night,

What dost thou think I have got ?

Fred. The pox, it may be.

John. Would 'twere no worse : you talk of
    revelations ;

I have got a revelation will reveal me

An errant coxcomb whilst I live.

VOL. I.   M   *Fred.*

Fred. What is't ?
Thou haſt loſt nothing ?

   John. No, I have got, I tell thee.

   Fred. What haſt thou got ?

   John. One of the infantry, a child.

   Fred. How ?

   John. A chopping child, man.

   Fred. Give you joy, Sir.

   John. A lump of lewdneſs, Frederick, that's
     the truth on't :
This town's abominable.

   Fred. I ſtill told ye, John,
Your whoring muſt come home ; I counſell'd you :
But, where no grace is-----

   John. 'Tis none of mine, man.

   Fred. Anſwer the pariſh ſo.

   John. Cheated in troth.
Peeping into a houſe, by vhom I know not,
Nor where to find the place again ; no, Frederick,
'Tis no poor one,
That's my beſt comfort, for't has brought about it
Enough to make it, man.

   Fred. Where is't ?

   John. At home.

   Fred. A ſaving voyage : but what will you ſay,
     Signior,

               To

To him that, fearching out your ferious worfhip,
Has met a ftranger fortune?

John. How, good Frederick?
A militant girl to this boy would hit it.

 Fred. No, mine's a nobler venture; what do
  you think, Sir,
Of a diftreffed lady, one whofe beauty
Would over-fell all Italy?

 John. Where is fhe?-----

 Fred. A woman of that rare behaviour,
So qualifi'd, as admiration
Dwells round about her; of that perfect fpirit----

 John. Ay marry, Sir!

 Fred. That admirable carriage,
That fweetnefs in difcourfe; young as the morning,
Her blufhes ftaining his.

 John. But where's this creature?
Shew me but that.

 Fred. That's all one, fhe's forth-coming,
I have her fure, boy.

 John. Hark ye, Frederick,
What truck betwixt my infant?

 Fred. 'Tis too light, Sir,
Stick to your charge, good Don John, I am well.

 John. But is there fuch a wench?

           Fred.

Fred. Firſt tell me this,
Did you not lately as you walk'd along,
Diſcover people that were armed and likely
To do offence?

   John. Yes marry, and they urg'd it as far as
      they had ſpirit.

   Fred. Pray go forward.

   John. A gentleman I found engag'd amongſt 'em;
It ſeems, of noble breeding, I'm ſure brave mettle,
As I return'd to look you, I ſet in to him,
And without hurt (I thank heaven) reſcu'd him.

   Fred. My work's done then:
And now to ſatisfy you, there is a woman,
Oh John! there is a woman------

   John. Oh where is ſhe?

   Fred. And one of no leſs worth, than I told ye;
And, which is more, fal'n under my protection.

   John. I am glad of that; forward, ſweet Frederick.

   Fred. And which is more than that, by this
      night's wandring,
And, which is moſt of all, ſhe is at home too, Sir.

   John. Come, let's be gone, then.

   Fred. Yes, but 'tis moſt certain,
You cannot ſee her, John.

   John. Why?

   Fred. She has ſworn me,

                   That

That none elſe ſhall come near her: not my mother,
Till ſome doubts are clear'd.

   John. Not look upon her! What chamber is
       ſhe in?

  Fred. In ours.

  John. Let's go, I ſay:
A woman's oaths are wafers, break with making,
They muſt for modeſty a little: we all know it.

   Fred. No, I'll aſſure you, Sir,

   John. Not ſee her?
I ſmell an old dog trick of yours. Well, Frederick,
You talk'd to me of whoring, let's have fair play,
Square dealing I would wiſh ye.

   Fred. When 'tis come
(Which I know never will be) to that iſſue,
Your ſpoon ſhall be as deep as mine, Sir.

   John. Tell me,
And tell me true, is the cauſe honourable?
Or for your eaſe?

   Fred. By all our friendſhip, John,
'Tis honeſt, and of great end.

   John. I am anſwer'd:
But let me ſee her tho'; leave the door open
As you go in.

   Fred. I dare not.

M 3

John.

John. Not wide open,
But juft fo, as a jealous hufband
Would level at his wanton wife through,
   Fred. That courtefy,
If ye defire no more, and keep it ftrictly,
I dare afford ye: come, 'tis now near morning,

                     [Exeunt.

S C E N E II.

Enter Peter *and* Anthony.

   Pet. Nay, the old woman's gone too.
   Ant. She's a catter-wauling
Amongft the gutters; but conceive ye, Peter,
Where our good mafters fhould be?
   Pet. Where they fhould be,
I do conceive, but where they are good Anthony---
   Ant. Ay, there it goes: my mafter's bo-peeps
      with' me,
With his fly popping in and out again,
Argu'd a caufe,---hark!   *[Lute founds.*
   Pet. What?
   Ant. Doft not hear a lute?
      Again!
   Pet. Where is't?
   Ant. Above, in my mafter's chamber.

                      Pet,

Pet. There's no creature: he hath the key
  himfelf, man.

Ant. This is his lute : let him have it.

                    [*Sing within a little.*

Pet. I grant you; but who ftrikes it?

Ant. An admirable voice too, hark you.

Pet. Anthony,

Art fure we are at home?

Ant. Without all doubt, Peter.

Pet. Then this muft be the devil.

Ant. Let it be.

Good devil fing again: O dainty devil?
Peter, believe it, a moft delicate devil,
The fweeteft devil——

      Enter Frederick *and* Don John.

 Fred. If you would leave peeping.

John. I cannot, by no means.

Fred. Then come in foftly;
And as you love your faith, prefume no farther
Than ye have promifed.

John. Bafco.

Fred. What make you up fo early, Sir?

John. You, Sir, in your contemplations!

Pet. O pray ye peace, Sir.

         M 4   *Fred.*

Fred. Why peace, Sir?

Pet. Do you hear?

John. 'Tis your lute.   She's playing on't.

Ant. The houfe is haunted, Sir;
For this we have heard this half year.

Fred. Ye faw nothing?

Ant. Not I.

Pet. Nor I, Sir.

Fred. Get you our breakfaft then,
And make no words on't; we'll undertake this fpirit,
If it be one.

Ant. This is no devil, Peter,
Mum, there be bats abroad.   [*Exeunt ambo.*

Fred. Stay, now fhe fings.

John. An angels voice I'll fwear.

Fred. Why did'ft thou fhrug fo?
Either allay this heat; or as I live
I will not truft you.

John. Pafs; I warrant ye.   [*Exeunt.*

Enter 1ft Conftantia.

Con. To curfe thofe ftars that men fay govern us,
To rail at fortune, to fall out with fate,
And tax the gen'ral world, will help me nothing:
Alas! I am the fame ftill, neither are they
                                        Subject

Subject to helps or hurts; our own defires
Are our own fates; our own ftars, all our fortunes,
Which, as we fway 'em, fo abufe or blefs us.

Enter Frederick, *and* Don John *peeping.*

Fred. Peace to your meditations.

John. Pox upon you,
Stand out o' th' light.

Con. I crave your mercy, Sir;
My mind o'ercharged with care made me unmannerly.

Fred. Pray you fet that mind at reft, all fhall
be perfect.

John. I like the body rarely; a handfome body,
A wondrous handfome body; would fhe would turn:
See, and that fpightful puppy be not got
Between me and my light again.

Fred. 'Tis done,
As all that you command fhall be: the gentleman
Is fafely off all danger.

John. Rare creature!

Con. How fhall I thank you, Sir? how fatisfy?

Fred. Speak foftly, gentle lady, all's rewarded;
Now does he melt like marmalade.   [*afide.*

John. Nay, 'tis certain,

Thou

Thou art the fweeteſt woman, that eyes e'er
    look'd on.

Fred. Has none diſturb'd you ?

Con. Not any, Sir, nor any found come near me,
I thank your care.

Fred. 'Tis well.

John. I would fain pray now,   [*aſide.*
But the devil, and that fleſh there, O th' world !
What are we made to fuffer ?

Fred. He'll enter ;
Pull in your head and be hang'd.

John. Hark ye, Frederick,
I have brought you home your pack-faddle.

Fred. Pox upon you.

Con. Nay, let him enter : fie, my lord the duke,
Stand peeping at your friends !

Fred. You are cozen'd lady.
Here's no duke.

Con. I know him full well, Signior.

John. Hold thee there, wench.

Fred. This mad-brain'd fool will fpoil all.

Con. I do befeech your grace come in.

John. My grace !
There was a word of comfort.

                                    Fred.

Fred. Shall he enter,
Who e'er he be?
John. Well followed Frederick.
Con. With all my heart.

Enter Don John.

Fred. Come in then.
John. Blefs you lady.
Fred. Nay, ftart not, though he be a ftranger
    to you,
He's of a noble ftrain, my kinfman, lady,
My countryman, and fellow-traveller;
One bed contains us ever, one purfe feeds us,
And one faith free between us; do not fear him,
He's truly honeft.
John. That's a lye.   [*afide.*
Fred. And trufty:
Beyond your wifhes: valiant to defend,
And modeft to converfe with, as your blufhes.
John. Now may I hang myfelf; this commen-
    dation
Has broke the neck of all my hopes; for now
Muft I cry, no forfooth, and ay forfooth, and
    furely,
And truly as I live, and as I am honeft.
H'as done thefe things for nonce too; for he knows,
                                            Like

Like a moſt envious raſcal as he is,
I am not honeſt
This way: h'as watch'd his time,
But I ſhall quit him.

    Con. Sir, I credit you:

    Fred. Go ſalute her, John.

    John. Plague o' your commendations.

    Con. Sir, I ſhall now deſire to be a trouble.

    John. Never to me, ſweet lady, thus I ſeal
My faith, and all my ſervice.

    Con. One word, Signior.

    John. Now 'tis impoſſible I ſhould be honeſt.
What points ſhe at? my leg, I warrant; or
My well-knit body: ſit faſt, Don Frederick.

    Fred. 'Twas given him by that gentleman
You took ſuch care of, his own being loſt i'th'
        ſcuffle.

    Con. With much joy may he wear it: 'tis a right
        one,
I can aſſure you, gentlemen; and right happy
May he be in all fights, for that noble ſervice.

    Fred. Why do ye bluſh?

    Con. 'T had almoſt cozened me;
For not to lye, when I ſaw that, I look'd for
Another owner of it: but 'tis well.

                             Fred.

Fred. Who's there?   [*Knock within.*
Stand you a little clofe: come in, Sir.

Enter Anthony.

Now what's the news with you?

Ant. There is a gentleman without ·
Would fpeak with Don John.

John. Who, Sir?

Ant. I do not know, Sir, but he fhews a man
Of no mean reckoning.

John. Let him fhew his name,
And then return a little wifer.   [*Exit* Anthony.

Fred. How do you like her, John?

John. As well as you, Frederick,
For all I am honeft; you fhall find it too.

Fred. Art thou not honeft?

John. Art thou an afs?
" And modeft as her blufhes?" what a blockhead
Would e'er have popp'd out fuch a dry apology
For his dear friend? and to a gentlewoman,
A woman of her youth, and delicacy?
Thefe are arguments to draw them to abhor us.
An honeft moral man! 'tis for a conftable:
A handfome man, a wholefome man, a tough man,
A liberal man, a likely man, a man
                              · Made

Made up like Hercules, unflack'd with fervice:
The fame to-night, to-morrow night, the next
    night,
And fo to perpetuity of pleafures;
Thefe had been things to hearken to, things
    catching;
But you have fuch a fpic'd confideration,
Such qualms upon your worfhip's confcience,
Such chilblains in your blood, that all things
    prick you,
Which nature, and the liberal world makes cuftom;
And nothing but fair honour, O fweet honour!
Hang up your eunuch honour: that I was trufty,
And valiant, were things well put in; but modeft!
A modeft gentleman! O wit, where waft thou?

   Fred. I am forry, John.

   John. My lady's gentlewoman
Would laugh me to a fchool-boy, make me blufh
With playing with my cod-piece point: fy on thee,
A man of thy difcretion!

   Fred. It fhall be mended;
And henceforth you fhall have your due.

      Enter Anthony.

   John. I look for't: how now, who is't?

                  An

Ant. A gentleman of this city,
And calls himself Petruchio.

John. I'll attend him.

Enter Constantia.

Con. How did he call himself?

Fred. Petruchio,
Does it concern you ought?

Con. O gentlemen,
The hour of my destruction is come on me,
I am discover'd, lost, left to my ruin:
As ever ye ha' pity——

John. Do not fear,
Let the great devil come, he shall come through
    me first:
Lost here, and we about you!

Fred. Fall before us!

Con. O my unfortunate estate, all angers
Compar'd to his, to his——

Fred. Let his, and all men's,
Whil'st we have power and life, stand up for
    heaven's sake.

Con. I have offended heaven too; yet heaven
    knows——

John. We are all evil:

Yet heaven forbid: we should have our deserts.
What is he?

Con. Too, too near to my offence, Sir:
O he will cut me piece-meal.

Fred. 'Tis no treason?

John. Let it be what it will: if he cut here,
I'll find him cut-work.

Fred. He must buy you dear,
With more than common lives.

John. Fear not, nor weep:
By heaven I'll fire the town before you perish,
And then the more the merrier, we'll jog with you.

Fred. Come in, and dry your eyes.

John. Pray no more weeping,
Spoil a sweet face for nothing! my return
Shall end all this I warrant you.

Con. Heaven grant it may.

[*Exeunt.*

S C E N E III.

Enter Petruchio *with a letter.*

Petr. This man should be of quality and worth,
By Don Alvaro's letter; for he gives
No slight recommendations of him:
I'll e'en make use of him.

1   *Enter*

Enter Don John.

John. Save you, Sir: I am forry
My bufinefs was fo unmannerly, to make you
Wait thus long here.

Petr. Occafions muft be ferv'd, Sir:
But is your name Don John?

John. It is, Sir.

Petr. Then,
Firft for your own brave fake I muft embrace you:
Next, for the credit of your noble friend
Hernando de Alvaro, make ye mine:
Who lays his charge upon me in this letter
To look you out, and,
Whilft your occafions make you refident
In this place, to fupply you, love and honour you;
Which had I known fooner------

John. Noble Sir,
You'll make my thanks too poor : I wear a fword,
    Sir,
And have a fervice to be ftill difpos'd of,
As you fhall pleafe command it.

Petr. That manly courtefy is half my bufinefs, Sir,
And to be fhort, to make you know I honour you,
And in all points believe your worth-like oracle;
This day Petruchio,

A man that may command the ſtrength of this
    place,
Hazard the boldeſt ſpirits, hath made choice
Only of you, and in a noble office.
   John. Forward, I am free to entertain it.
   Petr. Thus then:
I do beſeech you mark me.
   John. I ſhall, Sir.
   Petr. Ferrara's duke, would I might call him
    worthy,
But that he has raz'd out from his family,
As he has mine with infamy.   This man,
Rather this powerful monſter, we being left
But two of all our houſe, to ſtock our memories,
My ſiſter Conſtantia and myſelf; with arts and
    witchcrafts,
Vows, and ſuch oaths heaven has no mercy for,
Drew to diſhonour this weak maid, by ſtealth,
And ſecret paſſages I knew not of;
Oft he obtain'd his wiſhes, oft abus'd her,
I am aſham'd to ſay the reſt: this purchas'd,
And his hot blood allay'd, he left her,
And all our name to ruin.
   John. This was foul play,
And ought to be rewarded ſo.

2

Petr.

Petr. I hope so;

He scap'd me yesternight:

Which if he dare again adventure for------

 John. Pray, Sir, what commands have you to

  lay on me?

 Petr. Only thus; by word of mouth to carry him

A challenge from me, that so, if he have honour

 in him,

We may decide all difference between us.

 John. Fair, and noble,

And I will do it home: When shall I visit you?

 Petr. Please you this afternoon, I will ride with

  you;

For, at a castle six miles hence, we are sure

To find him.

 John. I'll be ready.

 Petr. My man shall wait here,

To conduct you to my house.

 John. I shall not fail you, Sir. [*Exit* Petruchio.

Enter Frederick.

 Fred. How now?

 John. All's well, and better than thou could'st

expect, for this wench here is certainly no maid;

and I have hopes she is the same that our two

N 2   curious

curious coxcombs have been so long a-hunting after.

Fred. Why do ye hope so?

John. Why? becaufe firft she is no maid, and next becaufe she's handfome; there are two rea-fons for you: now do you find out a third, a better if you can. For take this, Frederick, for a cer-tain rule, fince she loves the fport, she'll never give it over; and therefore (if we have good luck) in time may fall to our shares.

Fred. Very pretty reafons indeed! But I thought you had known fome particular, that made you conclude this to be the woman.

John. Yes, I know her name is Conftantia.

Fred. That now is fomething; but I cannot be-lieve her difhoneft for all this: she has not one loofe thought about her.

John. It's no matter, she's loofe i'th' hilts, by heaven. There has been ftirring, fumbling with linen, Frederick.

Fred. There may be fuch a flip.

John. And will be, Frederick, whilft the old game's a-foot. I fear the boy, too, will prove hers I took up.

Fred. Good circumftances may cure all this yet.

I   *John.*

John. There thou hit'ft it, Frederick; come let's walk in, and comfort her ; that fhe is here is nothing yet fufpected. Anon I fhall tell thee why her brother came, (who, by this light, is a noble fellow) and what honour he has done to me, a ftranger, in calling me to ferve him. There be irons heating for fome, on my word, Frederick.

[*Exeunt.*

END OF THE SECOND ACT.

ACT III.   SCENE I.

Enter Landlady *and* Anthony.

Land. COME, Sir, who is it keeps your mafter company ?

Ant. I fay to you, Don John.

Land. I fay what woman ?

Ant. I fay fo too.

Land. I fay again I will know.

Ant. I fay 'tis fit you fhould.

Land. And I tell thee he has a woman here.

Ant. And I tell thee 'tis then the better for him.

Land. Was ever gentlewoman

N 3

So

So frumpt off with a fool? well, faucy Sirrah,
I will know who it is, and to what purpofe;
I pay the rent, and I will know how my houfe
Comes by thefe inflammations: if this geer hold,
Beft hang a fign-poft up, to tell the Signiors,
Here ye may have lewdnefs at livery.

Enter Frederick.

Ant. 'Twould be a great eafe to your age.
Fred. How now?
Why, what's the matter, landlady?
Land. What's the matter!
Ye ufe me decently among ye, gentlemen.
Fred. Who has abus'd her? you, Sir?
Land. Od's my witnefs,
I will not be thus treated, that I will not.
Ant. I gave her no ill language.
Land. Thou lyeft lewdly.
Thou took'ft me up at every word I fpoke,
As I had been a maukin, a flirt gillian;
And thou think'ft, becaufe thou canft write and read,
Our nofes muft be under thee.
Fred. Dare you, Sirrah?
Ant. Let but the truth be known, Sir, I befeech you;
She raves of wenches, and I know not what, Sir.
Land.

Land. Go too, thou know'ſt too well, thou wicked varlet,

Thou inſtrument of evil.

Ant. As I live, Sir, ſhe's ever thus till dinner.

Fred. Get you in, I'll anſwer you anon, Sir.

[*Exit* Anthony.

Now your grief, what is't? for I can gueſs-----

Land. You may, with ſhame enough,

If there were ſhame amongſt ye; nothing thought on,

But how ye may abuſe my houſe: not ſatisfied

With bringing home your baſtards to undo me,

But you muſt drill your whores here too; my patience,

Becauſe I bear, and bear, and carry all,

And as they ſay, am willing to groan under,

Muſt be your make-ſport now.

Fred. No more of theſe words,

No more murmurings, lady; for you know

That I know ſomething. I did ſuſpect your anger,

But turn it preſently and handſomely,

And bear yourſelf diſcreetly to this woman,

For ſuch a one there is indeed.

Land. 'Tis well, ſon.

N 4

Fred.

Fred. Leave off your devil's mattins, and your
    melancholies,
Or we fhall leave our lodgings.
    Land. You have much need
To ufe thefe vagrant ways, and to much profit:
You had that might content
(At home within yourfelves too) right good, gen-
    tlemen,
Wholefome, and you faid handfome. But you
    gallants,
Beaft that I was to believe you----
    Fred. Leave your fufpicion;
For as I live there's no fuch thing.
    Land. Mine honour;
And 'twere not for mine honour.
    Fred. Come, your honour,
Your houfe, and you too, if you dare believe me,
Are well enough : fleek up yourfelf, leave crying;
For I muft have ye entertain this lady
With all civility, fhe well deferves it,
Together with all fervice : I dare truft you,
For I have found you faithful: when you know her,
You will find your own fault ; no more words, but
    do it.
    Land. You know you may command me.
                                    Enter

Enter Don John.

John. Worfhipful lady,
How does thy velvet fcabbard? by this hand,
Thou lookeft moft amiably: now could I willingly
(And 'twere not for abufing thy Geneva print
     there,)
Venture my body with thee------

Land. You'll leave this roguery,
When you come to my years.

John. By this light,
Thou art not above fifteen yet, a meer girl,
Thou haft not half thy teeth------

Fred. Prithee, John,
Let her alone, fhe has been vex'd already:
She'll grow ftark mad, man.

John. I wou'd fain fee her mad,
An old mad woman------

Fred. Prithee be patient.

John. Is like a miller's mare, troubled wi'th'
     tooth-ach;
She makes the rareft faces.

Fred. Go, and do it,
And do not mind this fellow.

    [*Exit* Landlady, *and comes back again prefently.*
John. What, again!

                              Nay,

Nay, then it is decreed: though hills were fet on
    hills,
And feas met feas, to guard thee, I would through.

Land. Od's my witnefs, if ye ruffle me, I'll
fpoil your fweet face for you, that I will: go, go
to the door, there's a gentleman there would
fpeak with you.

John. Upon my life Petruchio; good, dear landlady, carry him into the dining-room, and I'll
wait upon him prefently:

Land, Well, Don John, the time will come that
I fhall be even with you.   *[Exit.*

John. I muft be gone: yet if my projeſt hold,
You fhall not ftay behind: I'll rather truft
A cat with fweet milk, Frederick; by her face,

Enter Conftantia.

I feel her fears are working.

Con. Is there no way,
I do befeech you, think yet, to divert
This certain danger?

Fred. 'Tis impoffible:
Their honours are engag'd.

Con. Then there muft be murder,
Which, gentlemen, I fhall no fooner hear of,

Than

Than make one in't: you may, if you pleafe, Sir,
Make all go lefs------

John. Lady, were't mine own caufe,
I could difpenfe; but loaden with my friends truft,
I muft go on, though general maffacres,
As much I fear------

Con. Do ye hear, Sir? for heaven's fake,
Let me requeft one favour of you.

Fred. Yes, any thing.

Con. This gentleman I find is too refolute,
Too hot and fiery for the caufe: as ever
You did a virtuous deed, for honour's fake,
Go with him and allay him: your fair temper,
A noble difpofition, like wifh'd fhowers,
May quench thofe eating fires, that would fpoil
    all elfe.
I fee in him deftruction.

Fred. I will do it, and 'tis a wife confideration,
To me a bounteous favour: hark ye John,
I will go with ye.

John. No.

Fred. Indeed I will,
You go upon a hazard; no denial?
For as I live I'll go.

                       John.

John. Then make ye ready, .
For I am ftrait on horfe-back.

Fred. My fword on, and
I am as ready as you: what my beft labour,
With all the art I have can work upon 'em,
Be fure of, and expect a fair end: the old gentle-
　　woman
Shall wait upon ye; fhe is difcreet and fecret,
You may truft her in all points.

Con. Ye are noble;
And fo I take my leave.

John. I hope, lady, a happy iffue for all this.

Con. All heaven's care upon ye, and my prayers.

John. So,
Now my mind's at reft,

Fred. Away, 'tis late, John.　　　　　*[Exeunt.*

S C E N E II.

Enter Antonio, Surgeon, *and a* Gentleman.

Gent. What fymptoms do you find in him?

Sur. None, Sir, dangerous, if he'd be rul'd:

Gent. Why! what does he do?

Sur. Nothing that he fhould. Firft, he will let
no liquor down but wine, and then he has a fancy
　　　　　　　　　　　　　　that

that he muſt be dreſt always to the tune of John
Dory:

Gent. How to the tune of John Dory?

Sur. Why, he will have fidlers, and make them
play and ſing it to him all the while.

Gent. An odd fancy indeed.

Ant. Give me ſome, wine.

Sur. I told you ſo------'Tis death, Sir:

Ant. 'Tis a horſe, Sir. Doſt think I ſhall reco-
ver with the help of barley-water only?

Gent. Fy, Antonio, you muſt be govern'd.

Ant. Why, Sir, he feeds me with nothing but
rotten roots, and drown'd chickens, ſtew'd *Peri-
craniums*, and *Pia-maters*; and when I go to bed,
(by heaven 'tis true, Sir) he rolls me up in lints
with labels at 'em, that I am juſt the man i' th'
almanack; my head and face is *Aries* place.

Sur. Will't pleaſe you to let your friends ſee
       you open'd?

Ant. Will't pleaſe you, Sir, to give me a brimmer? I feel my body open enough for that.
Give it me, or I'll die upon thy hand, and ſpoil
thy cuſtom.

Sur. How, a brimmer?

Ant. Why, look ye, Sir, thus I am us'd ſtill;

I can

I can get nothing that I want. In how long time canſt thou cure me?

Sur. In forty days.

Ant. I'll have a dog ſhall lick me whole in twenty.
In how long canſt thou kill me?

Sur. Preſently.

Ant. Do't, that's the ſhorter, and there's more
    delight in't.

Gent. You muſt have patience.

Ant. Man, I muſt have buſineſs; this fooliſh fellow hinders himſelf; I have a dozen raſcals to
hurt within theſe five days. Good man-mender,
ſtop me up with parſly like ſtuff'd beef, and let
me walk abroad.

Sur. Ye ſhall walk ſhortly.

Ant. I will walk preſently, Sir, and leave your
ſalads there, your green ſalves and your oils; I'll
to my old diet again, ſtrong food, and rich wine,
and try what that will do.

Sur. Well, go thy ways, thou art the maddeſt
old fellow I e'er yet met with   [*Exeunt.*

SCENE

SCENE III.

Enter Conſtantia *and* Landlady.

Con. I have told you all I can, and more than yet
Thoſe gentlemen know of me ; but are they
Such ſtrange creatures, ſay you ?

Land. There's the younger,
Don John, the errant'ſt Jack in all this city :
The other, time has blaſted, yet he will ſtoop,
If not o'erflown, and freely on the quarry ;
H'as been a dragon in his days. But Tarmont,
Don Jenkin, is the devil himſelf, the dog-days,
The moſt incomprehenſive whoremaſter,
Twenty a night is nothing : the truth is,
Whoſe chaſtity he chops upon, he cares not.
He flies at all ; baſtards upon my conſcience,
He has now in making multitudes : the laſt night
He brought home one ; I pity her that bore it,
But we are all weak veſſels.. Some rich woman
(For wife I dare not call her) was the mother,
For it was hung with jewels ; the bearing cloth
No leſs than crimſon velvet.

Con. How ?

Land. 'Tis true, lady.

Con. Was it a boy too ?

Land.

Land. A brave boy ; deliberation
And judgment fhew'd in's getting, as I'll fay for him,
He's as well pac'd for that fpo. t-----

Con. May I fee it ?

For there is a neighbour of mine, a gentlewoman,
Has had a late mifchance, which willingly
I would know further of; now if you pleafe
To be fo courteous to me.

Land. Ye fhall fee it :

But what do you think of thefe men, now you
     know 'em ?

Be wife,

You may repent too late elfe ; I but tell you
For your own good, and as you will find it, lady.

Con. I am advis'd.

Land. No more words then ; do that,
And inftantly, I told you of; be ready.
Don John, I'll fit you for your frumps.

Con. But fhall I fee this child ?

Land. Within this half hour :

Let's in, and there think better.   [*Exeunt.*

SCENE IV.

Enter Petruchio, Don John *and* Frederick.

John. Sir, he is worth your knowledge, and a
    gentleman   (If

(If I that fo much love him may commend him)
That's full of honour; and one, if foul play
Should fall upon us, for which fear I brought him,
Will not fly back for fillips.

Petr. Ye much honour me,
And once more I pronounce ye both mine.

Fred. Stay, what troop
Is that below i' th' valley there?

John. Hawking, I take it.

Petr. They are fo; 'tis the duke, 'tis even.he,
      gentlemen :
Sirrah, draw back the horfes till we call ye,
I know him by his company.

Fred. I think too
He bends up this way.

Petr. So he does.

John. Stand you ftill
Within that covert, till I call: he comes
Forward; here will I wait him: to your places.

Petr. I need no more inftruct you.

John. Fear me not.   [*Exeunt* Petr. *and* Fred.
      Enter Duke *and his faction.*

Duke. Feed the hawks up,
We'll fly no more to day: O my bleft fortune!
Have I fo fairly met the man?

John. Ye have, Sir,
And him you know by this.

Duke. Sir, all the honour,
And love------

John. I do befeech your grace ftay there, and
Difmifs your train a little.

Duke. Walk afide,
And out of hearing, I command you;
Now, Sir, be plain.

John. I will, and fhort;
Ye have wrong'd a gentleman, beyond all juftice,
Beyond the mediation of all friends.

Duke. The man, and manner of wrong?

John. Petruchio;
The wrong, you have difhonoured his fifter.

Duke. Now ftay you, Sir,
And hear me a little : this gentleman's
Sifter that you nam'd, 'tis true, I have long lov'd;
As true I have enjoy'd her : no lefs truth
I have a child by her. But that fhe, or he,
Or any of that family are tainted,
Suffer difgrace or ruin, by my pleafures,
I wear a fword to fatisfy the world no,
And him in this caufe when he pleafes: for know, Sir,
She is my wife, contracted before heaven,

(A witnefs

(A witnefs I owe more tye to, than her brother)
Nor will I fly from that name, which long fince
Had had the churches approbation,
But for his jealous nature.

    John. Your pardon, Sir ; I am fully fatisfied.

    Duke. Dear, Sir, I knew I fhould convert you;
       had we
But that rough man here now too----

    John. And you fhall, Sir,
What, hoa, hoa,

    Duke. I hope you have laid no ambufh?

Enter Petruchio.

    John. Only friends.

    Duke. My noble brother welcome :
Come put your anger off, we'll have no fighting,
Unlefs you will maintain I am unworthy
To bear that name.

    Petr. Do you fpeak this heartily?

    Duke. Upon my foul, and truly ; the firft prieft
Shall put you out of thefe doubts.

    Petr. Now I love you,
And I befeech ye pardon my fufpicions ;
You are now more than a brother, a brave friend too.

    John. The good man's overjoy'd.

Enter Frederick.

Fred. How now, how goes it?

John. Why, the man has his mare again, and
　　all's well.

The duke profeſſes freely he's her huſband.

Fred. 'Tis a good hearing.

John. Yes, for a modeſt gentleman: I muſt pre-
　　ſent you;

May it pleaſe your grace,

To number this brave gentleman, my friend,

And noble kinſman, amongſt the reſt of your
　　ſervants.

Duke. O my brave friend; you ſhower your
　　bounties on me.

Amongſt my beſt thoughts, Signior; in which
　　number

You being worthily diſpos'd already,

May freely place your friend.

Fred. Your grace does me a great deal of honour.

Petr. Why this is wondrous happy: but now,
　　brother,

Now comes the bitter to our ſweet: Conſtantia.

Duke. Why, what of her?

Petr. Nor what, nor where do I know;

　　　　　　　　　　　　Wing'd

Wing'd with her fears, laſt night, beyond my
    knowledge,
She quit my houſe, but whether------
   Fred. Let not that------
   Duke. No more, good Sir, I have heard too
    much.
   Petr. Nay, ſink not,
She cannot be ſo loſt.
   John. Nor ſhall not ; gentlemen,
Be free again, the lady's found ; that ſmile, Sir,
Shows you diſtruſt your ſervant.
   Duke. I do beſeech you.
   John. You ſhall believe me, by my ſoul ſhe's ſafe.
   Fred. You may ſafely.
   John. And under noble uſage : this gentleman
Met her in all her doubts laſt night, and to his
    guard
(Her fears being ſtrong upon her) ſhe gave her
   . perſon,
Who waited on her to our lodging, where all refpeÃt,
Civil and honeſt ſervice now attend her.
   Petr. You may believe now.
   Duke. Yes I do, and ſtrongly ;
Well, my good friends, or rather my good angels,
O 3   For

For you have both preferv'd me; when thefe virtues
Die in your friends remembrance------

John. Good your grace,
Lofe no more time in compliments, 'tis too precious;
I know it myfelf, there can be no hell
To his that hangs upon his hopes.

Petr. He has hit it.

Fred. To horfe again then, for this night I'll crown
With all the joys you wifh for.

Petr. Happy gentlemen.   [*Exeunt.*

Enter Francifco, *and a* Man.

Fran. This is the maddeft mifchief, never fool
was ever fo fubb'd off as I am, made ridiculous,
and to myfelf, to my own afs; truft a woman, I'll
truft the devil firft, for he dares be better than his
word fometimes. Pray tell me, in what obfervance
have I e'er fail'd her?

Man. Nay, you can tell that beft yourfelf.

Fran. Let me confider.

Enter Don Frederick *and* Don John.

Fred. Let them talk, we'll go on before.

Fran. Where didft thou meet Conftantia, and
this woman?

Fred.

Fred. Conftantia! What are thefe fellows? ftay, by all means.

Man. Why, Sir, I met her in the great ftreet that comes from the market-place, juft at the turning by a goldfmith's fhop.

Fred. Stand ftill, John.

Fran. Well, Conftantia has fpun herfelf a fair thread now :
What will her beft friend think of this?

Fred. John, I fmell fome juggling, John.

John. Yes, Frederick, I fear it will be proved fo.

Fran. But what fhould the reafon be, doft think, of this fo fudden change in her?

Fred. 'Tis fhe.

Man. Why, truly I fufpect fhe has been entic'd to it by a ftranger:

John. Did you mark that, Frederick?

Fran. Stranger! Who?

Man. A young gentleman that's newly come to town.

Fred. Mark that too.

John. Yes, Sir.

Fran. Why do you think fo?

Man. I heard her grave conductrefs twattle fomething as they went along, that makes me guefs it.

John.

John. 'Tis fhe, Frederick.

Fred. But who that He is, John.

Fran. I do not doubt to bolt 'em out, for they muft certainly be about the town. Ha! no more words? come, let's be gone.

[*Exeunt* Fran. *and* Man.

Fred. Well.

John. Very well.

Fred. Difcreetly.

John. Finely carried.

Fred. You have no more of thefe tricks?

John. Ten to one, Sir, I fhall meet with 'em if you have.

Fred. Is this fair?

John. Was it in you a friend's part to deal double? I am no afs, Don Frederick.

Fred. And, Don John, it fhall appear I am no fool: difgrace me to make yourfelf thus every woman's courtefy? 'tis boyifh, 'tis bafe.

John. 'Tis falfe; I privy to this dog-trick? clear yourfelf, for I know well enough where the wind fits; or as I have a life---- [*Trampling within.*

Fred. No more, they are coming; fhew no dif-content, let's quietly away; if fhe be at home, our jealoufies

jealoufies are over ; if not, you and I muft have a
farther parly, John.

John. Yes, Don Frederick, you may be fure we
fhall : but where are thefe fellows? pox on't, we
have loft them too in our fpleen, like fools.

Enter Duke *and* Petruchio.

Duke. Come, gentlemen, let's go a little fafter ;
Suppofe you have all miftreffes, and mend
Your pace accordingly.

John. Sir, I fhould be as glad of a miftrefs as
    another man.

Fred. Yes, o'my confcience would'ft thou, and
of any other man's miftrefs too; that I'll anfwer
for.   [*Exeunt.*

S C E N E · V.

Enter Antonio *and his* Man.

Ant. With all my gold ?

Man. The trunk broken open, and all gone.

Ant. And the mother in the plot ?

Man. And the mother and all.

Ant. And the devil and all : the mighty pox go
with 'em; belike they thought I was no more of
                                  this

this world, and thofe trifles would but difturb my confcience.

Man. Sure they thought, Sir, you wou'd not live to difturb them.

Ant. Well, my fweet miftrefs, I'll try how hand-fomely your ladyfhip can hang upon a pair of gallows; there's your mafter-piece. No imagination where they fhould be?

Man. None Sir; yet we have fearch'd all places we fufpected: I believe they have taken towards the port.

Ant. Get me then a water-conjurer, one that can raife water-devils, I'll port 'em; play at duck and drake with my money! get me a conjurer, I fay, enquire out a man that lets out devils.

Man. I don't know where.

Ant. In every ftreet, Tom Fool, any blear'd ey'd people with red heads, and flat nofes, can perform it. Thou fhalt know 'em by their half gowns, and no breeches. Find me out a conjurer, I fay, and learn his price, how he will let his devils out by the day. I'll have 'em again if they be above ground.   [*Exeunt.*

SCENE

SCENE VI.

Enter Duke, Petruchio, Frederick, *and* John.

Petr. Your grace is welcome now to Bologna; so you are all, gentlemen.

John. Don Frederick, will you ſtep in, and give the lady notice who comes to viſit her?

Petr. Bid her make haſte; we come to ſee no curious wench, a night gown will ſerve turn. Here's one that knows her nearer.

Fred. I'll tell her what you ſay, Sir.   [*Exit.*

Petr. Now will the ſport be to obſerve her alterations, how betwixt fear and joy ſhe will behave herſelf.

Duke. Dear brother, I muſt entreat you----

Petr. I conceive your mind, Sir, I will not chide her.

Enter Frederick *and* Peter.

John. How now?

Fred. You may, Sir; not to abuſe your patience longer, nor hold you off with tedious circumſtances; for you muſt know------

Petr. What?

Duke. Where is ſhe?

Fred. Gone, Sir.

Duke.

Duke. How!

Petr. What did you fay, Sir ?

Fred. Gone, by heaven remov'd. The woman of the houfe too.

Petr. What, that reverend old woman that tir'd me with compliments ?

Fred. The very fame.

John. Well, Don Frederick.

Fred. Don John, it is not well. But------

Petr. Gone!

Fred. This fellow can fatisfy I lye not.

Pet. A little after my mafter was departed, Sir, with this gentleman, my fellow and myfelf being fent on bufinefs, as we muft think on purpofe.----

Petr. Hang thefe circumftances, they always ferve to ufher in ill ends.

John. Now could I eat that rogue, I am fo angry. Gone!

Petr. Gone!

Fred. Directly gone, fled, fhifted; what would you ha' me fay ?

Duke. Well, gentlemen, wrong not my good opinion.

Fred. For your dukedom, Sir, I would not be a knave.

John.

John. He that is, a rot run in his blood.

Petr. But hark you, gentlemen, are you fure you had her here? did you not dream this?

John. Have you your nofe, Sir?

Petr. Yes, Sir.

John. Then we had her.

Petr. Since you are fo fhort, believe your having her fhall fuffer more conftruction.

John. Well, Sir, let it fuffer.

Fred. How to convince you, Sir, I can't imagine; but my life fhall juftify my innocence, or fall with it.

Duke. Thus then——for we may be all abus'd.

Petr. 'Tis poffible.

Duke. Here let's part until to-morrow this time; we to our way to clear this doubt, and you to yours: pawning our honours then to meet again; when if fhe be not found——

Fred. We ftand engag'd to anfwer any worthy way we are call'd to.

Duke. We afk no more.

Petr. To morrow certain.

John. If we out-live this night, Sir.

[*Exeunt* Duke *and* Petruchio.

Fred.

Fred. Come, Don John, we have fomewhat now
to do.

John. I am fure I would have.

Fred. If fhe be not found, we muft fight.

John. I am glad on't, I have not fought a great
while.

Fred. If we die------

John. There's fo much money fav'd in lechery.

[*Exeunt.*

END OF THE THIRD ACT.

ACT IV.   SCENE I.

Enter 2d Conftantia *and her* Mother.

Moth. HOLD, Cons, hold, for goodnefs hold;
I am in that defertion of fpirit for want of breath,
that I am almoft reduc'd to the neceffity of not
being able to defend myfelf againft the inconve-
nience of a fall.

2 Con. Dear mother, let us go a little fafter to
fecure ourfelves from Antonio; for my part I am
in that terrible fright, that I can neither think,
fpeak, nor ftand ftill, till we are fafe on fhip-
board, and out of fight of the fhore.

Moth.

Moth. Out of fight o'the fhore! why, do you
think I'll depatriate?

2 *Con.* Depatriate! what's that?

Moth. Why, you fool you, leave my country:
what, will you never learn to fpeak out of the vulgar road?

2 *Con.* O lord! this hard word will undo us.

Moth. As I am a chriftian, if it were to fave my
honour, (which is ten thoufand times dearer to me
than my life) I would not be guilty of fo odious a
thought.

2 *Con.* Pray mother, fince your honour is fo
dear to you, confider that, if we are taken, both
it and we are loft for ever.

Moth. Ay, girl, but what will the world fay, if
they fhould hear fo odious a thing of us, as that
we fhould depatriate?

2 *Con.* Ay, there's it; the world! why, mother,
the world does not care a pin if both you and I
were hang'd; and that we fhall be certainly, if
Antonio takes us, for running away with his gold.

Moth. Proteft I care not, I'll ne'er depart from
the demarches of a perfon of quality; and let
come what will, I fhall rather choofe to fubmit
myfelf to my fate, than ftrive to prevent it by any

I   deportment

.deportment that is not congruous, in every degree; to the steps and measures of a strict practitioner of honour.

2. *Con.* Would not this make one start mad ? her stile is not more out of the way, than her manner of reasoning; she first sells me to an ugly old fellow, then she runs away with me and all his gold, and now, like a strict practitioner of honour, resolves to be taken, rather than depatriate, as she calls it.   [*Aside.*

Moth. As I am a christian, Cons, a tavern, and a very decent sign ! I'll in, I am resolv'd, though by it I should run a risco of never so stupenduous a nature.

2 *Con.* There's no stopping her; what shall I do ?

Moth. I'll send for my kinswoman, and some musick, to revive me a little; for really, Cons, I am reduc'd to that sad imbecillity by the injury I have done my poor feet, that I'm in a great incertitude whether they will have livelinefs sufficient to support me up to the top of the stairs or no. [*Exit.*

2 *Con.* This sinning without pleasure I cannot endure; to have always a remorse, and ne'er do any thing that should cause it, is intolerable. If I lov'd money too, which, I think, I don't, my

mother

mother fhe has all that: I have nothing to comfort myfelf with but Antonio's ftiff beard; and that alone, for a woman of my years, is but a forry kind of entertainment. I wonder why thefe old fumbling fellows fhould trouble themfelves fo much, only to trouble us more. They can do nothing, but put us in mind of our graves. Well, I'll no more on't; for to be frighted with death and damnation, both at once, is a little too hard. I do here vow I'll live for ever chafte, or find out fome handfome young fellow I can love; I think that's the better; [*Mother looks out at the window.*

Moth. Come up, Cons, the fiddles are here.

2 *Con.* I come----[*Mother goes from the window.* I muft be gone, tho' whither I cannot tell; thefe fiddlers, and her difcreet companions will quickly make an end of all fhe has ftolen, and then for 500 new pieces fell me to another old fellow. She has taken care not to leave me a farthing; yet I am fo, better than under her conduct: 'twill be at worft but begging for my life.

And ftarving were to me an eafier fate,
Than to be forc'd to live with one I hate.

[*Goes up to her mother.*

SCENE II.

Enter Don John.

John. It will not out of my head, but that Don
Frederick has fent away this wench, for all he car-
ries it fo gravely; yet methinks he fhould be
honefter than fo: but thefe grave men are never
touch'd upon fuch occafions. Mark it when you
will, and you'll find a grave man, efpecially if he
pretend to be a precife man, will do you forty
things without remorfe, that would ftartle one of
us mad fellows to think of: becaufe they are familiar with heaven in their prayers, they think
they may be bold with it in any thing: now we,
that are not fo well acquainted, bear greater reve-
rence.   [*Mufick plays above.*
What's here, mufick and women? would I had
one of em.   [*One of 'em looks out of the window.*
That's a whore; I know her by her fmile. O'my
confcience, take a woman mafked and hooded;
nay, cover'd all o'er, fo that you cannot fee one bit
of her, and at twelve fcore yards diftance, if fhe be
a whore, as ten to one fhe is, I fhall know it certainly: I have an inftinct within me never fails.
      [*Another looks out.*
Ah rogue! fhe's right too, I'm fure on't.
        Moth.

Moth. above. Come, come, let's dance in t'other room, 'tis a great deal better.

John. Say you fo? what now if I fhould go up and dance too? It is a tavern, pox o' this bufinefs; I'll in, I am refolved, and try my own fortune; 'tis hard luck if I don't get one of 'em.

As he goes to the door, 2d Conftantia *enters.* See here's one bolted already: fair lady, whither fo faft?

2 Con. I don't know, Sir.

John. May I have the honour to wait upon you?

2 Con. Yes, if you pleafe, Sir.

John. Whither?

2 Con. I tell you I don't know.

John. She's very quick: would I might be fo happy as to know you, lady.

2 Con. I dare not let you fee my face, Sir.

John. Why?

2 Con. For fear you fhould not like it, and then leave me; for to tell you true, I have at this prefent very great need of you.

John. If thou haft half fo much need of me, as I have of thee, lady, I'll be content to be hang'd tho'.

2 Con. It's a proper handfome fellow this: if

he'd

he'd but love me now, I would never feek out farther. Sir, I am young, and unexperienc'd in the world.

John. Nay, if thou art young, it's no great matter what thy face is.

2 *Con.* Perhaps this freedom in me may feem ftrange; but, Sir, in fhort, I'm forc'd to fly from one I hate: if I fhould meet him, will you here promife he fhall not take me from you?

John. Yes, that I will, before I fee your face, your fhape has charm'd me enough for that already; if any one takes you from me, lady, I'll give him leave to take from me too-----(I was a-going to name 'em) certain things of mine, that I would not lofe, now I have you in my arms, for all the gems in Chriftendom.

2 *Con.* For heaven's fake then conduct me to fome place, where I may be fecured a while from the fight of any one whatfoever.

John. By all the hopes I have to find thy face as lovely as thy fhape, I will.

2 *Con.* Well, Sir, I believe you; for you have au honeft look.

John. 'Slid I am afraid, Don Frederick has been
given

giving her a character of me too. Come, pray unmaſk.

2 Con. Then turn away your face; for I'm re-ſolv'd you ſhall not ſee a bit of mine, till I have ſet it in order, and then-----

John. What?

2 Con. I'll ſtrike you dead.

John. A mettled whore, I warrant her: come, if ſhe be now young, and have but a noſe on her face, ſhe'll be as good as her word. I'm e'en panting for breath already.

2 Con. Now ſtand your ground if you dare.

John. By this light a rare creature! ten thou-ſand times handſomer than her we ſeek for! this can be ſure no common one: pray heaven ſhe be not a whore.

2 Con. Well, Sir, what ſay you now?

John. Nothing, I'm ſo amaz'd, I am not able to ſpeak. I'd beſt fall too preſently, though it be in the ſtreet, for fear of loſing time: pr'ythee, my dear ſweet creature, go with me into that corner, that thou and I may talk a little in private.

2 Con. No, Sir, no private dealing, I beſeech you.

John. 'Sheart, what ſhall I do? I'm out of my

P 3

wit.

wits for her. Hark you, my dear foul, canft thou
love me?

2 Con. If I could, what then ?

John. Why, you know what then, and then
fhould I be the happieft man alive.

2 Con. Ay, fo you all fay till you have your
defires, and then you leave us.

John. But, my dear heart, I am not made like
other men; I never can love heartily till I have----

2 Con. Got their maidenheads; but fuppofe now
I fhould be no maid.

John. Pr'ythee fuppofe me nothing, but let me
try.

2 Con. Nay, good Sir, hold.

John. No maid! why, fo much the better, thou
art then the more experienc'd; for my part I hate
a bungler at any thing.

2 Con. O dear! I like this fellow ftrangely:
hark you, Sir, I am not worth a groat; but though
you fhould not be fo neither, if you'll but love me,
I'll follow you all the world over; I'll work for
you, beg for you, do any thing for you, fo you'll
promife to do nothing with any body elfe.

John. O heaven's! I'm in another world, this
wench fure was made o'purpofe for me, fhe is fo

juft

just of my humour. My dear, 'tis impossible for me to say how much I will do for thee, or with thee, thou sweet bewitching woman; but let's make haste home, or I shall never be able to hold out till I come thither. [*Exeunt.*

SCENE III.

Enter Frederick *and* Francisco.

Fred. And art thou sure it was Constantia, say'st thou, that he was leading?

Fran. Am I sure I live, Sir? Why, I dwelt in the house with her; how can I chuse but know her?

Fred. But did'st thou see her face?

Fran. Lord, Sir, I saw her face as plainly as I see yours just now, not two streets off.

Fred. Yes, 'tis e'en so; I suspected it at first, but then he forswore it with that confidence———— Well, Don John, if these be your practices, you shall have no more a friend of me, Sir, I assure you. Perhaps, tho', he met her by chance, and intends to carry her to her brother, and the duke.

Enter Don John, *and second* Constantia.

A little time will shew.-----Gods so, here he is;

I'll

I'll ſtep behind this ſhop, and obſerve what he ſays.

John. Here, now go in, and make me for ever happy.

Fred. Dear Don John.

John. A pox o' your kindneſs, how the devil comes he here juſt at this time? now will he aſk me forty fooliſh queſtions, and I have ſuch a mind to this wench, that I cannot think of one excuſe, for my life.

Fred. Your ſervant, Sir; pray who's that you lock'd in juſt now at the door?

John. Why, a friend of mine that's gone up to read a book.

Fred. A book! that's a queint one, i'faith: pr'ythee, Don John, what library haſt thou been buying this afternoon? for i'th'morning to my knowledge thou had'ſt never a book there, except it were an almanack, and that was none of thy own neither.

John. No, no, it's a book of his own he brought along with him. A ſcholar that is given to reading.

Fred. And do ſcholars, Don John, wear petticoats now a-days?

John.

John. Plague on him, he has feen her.—-Well, Don Frederick, thou know'ft I am not good at lying; 'tis a woman, I confefs it, make your beft on't, what then?

Fred. Why then, Don John, I defire you'll be pleas'd to let me fee her.

John. Why, faith, Frederick, I fhould not be againft the thing, but you know a man muft keep his word, and fhe has a mind to be private.

Fred. But, John, you may remember when I met a lady fo before, this very felf-fame lady too, that I got leave for you to fee her John.

John. Why, do you think then that this here is Conftantia?

Fred. I cannot properly fay I think it, John, be-caufe I know it; this fellow here faw her as you led her i'th' ftreets.

John. Well, and what then? who does he fay it is?

Fred. Afk him, Sir, and he'll tell you.

John. Sweet-heart, doft thou know this lady?

Fran. I think I fhould, Sir, I ha' liv'd long enough in the houfe with her to know her fure.

John. And how do they call her pr'ythee?

Fran. Conftantia!

John.

John. How! Conftantia!

Fran. Yes, Sir, the woman's name is Conftantia; that's flat.

John. Is it fo, Sir? and fo is this too. [*Strikes him.*
Fran. Oh, oh.   [*Runs out.*
John. Now, Sirrah, you may fafely fay you have not born falfe witnefs for nothing.

Fred. Fy, Don John, why do you beat the poor fellow for doing his duty, and telling truth?

Frea. Telling truth! thou talk'ft as if thou hadft been hir'd to bear falfe witnefs too: you are a very fine gentleman.

Fred. What a ftrange confidence he has! but is there no fhame in thee? nor any confideration of what is juft, or honeft, to keep a woman thus againft her will, that thou know'ft is in love with another man too; do'ft think a judgment will not follow this?

John. Good dear Frederick, do thou keep thy fentences and thy morals for fome better opportunity, this here is not a fit fubject for 'em: I tell thee fhe is no more Conftantia than thou art.

Fred. Why won't you let me fee her then?

John. Becaufe I can't; befides, fhe is not for thy turn.

Fred.

Fred. How fo?

John. Why, thy genius lies another way; thou art for flames, and darts, and thofe fine things; now I am for the old plain down-right way; I am not fo curious, Frederick, as thou art.

Fred. Very well, Sir; but is this worthy in you, to endeavour to debauch------

John. But is there no fhame? but is this worthy? what a many buts are here! if I fhould tell thee now folemnly thou haft but one eye, and give thee reafons for it, would'ft thou believe me?

Fred. I think hardly, Sir, againft my own know-ledge.

John. Then why doft thou, with that grave face, go about to perfuade me againft mine? you fhould do as you would be done by, Frederick.

Fred. And fo I will, Sir, in this very particular, fince there's no other remedy; I fhall do that for the Duke and Petruchio, which I fhould expect from them upon the like occafion: In fhort, to let you fee I am as fenfible of my honour, as you can be carelefs of yours; I muft tell you, Sir, that I'm refolv'd to wait upon this lady to them.

John. Are you fo, Sir? why, I muft then, fweet Sir, tell you again, I am refolved you fhan't. Ne'er
ftare,

ftare, nor wonder, I have promis'd to preferve her from the fight of any one whatfoever, and with the hazard of my life will make it good; but that you may not think I mean an injury to Petruchio, or the Duke, know, Don Frederick, that though I love a wench perhaps a little better, I hate to do a thing that's bafe, as much as you do. Once more upon my honour, this is not Conftantia; let that fatisfy you.

Fred. All that will not do------[*Goes to the door.*

John. No? Why then this fhall. (*draws.*) Come not one ftep nearer, for if thou do'ft, by heaven it is thy laft.

Fred. This is an infolence beyond the temper of a man to fuffer------thus I throw off thy friend-fhip, and fince thy folly has provok'd my patience beyond its natural bounds, know it is not in thy power now to fave thyfelf.

John. That's to be try'd, Sir, tho', by your favour. (*Looks up to the window.*) Miftrefs what you call 'em-----pr'ythee look now a little, and fee how I'll fight for thee.

Fred. Come, Sir, are you ready?

John. O Lord, Sir, your fervant.   [*Fight.*

SCENE.

SCENE IV.

Enter Duke *and* Petruchio.

Petr. What's here, fighting? let's part 'em: How? Don Frederick againſt Don John! how came you to fall out, gentlemen? What's the cauſe?

Fred. Why, Sir, it is your quarrel, and not mine, that drew this on me: I ſaw him lock Conſtantia up into that houſe, and I deſired to wait upon her to you; that's the cauſe.

Duke. O, it may be he deſign'd to lay the obligation upon us himſelf; Sir, we are beholden to you for this favour, beyond all poſſibility of----

John. Pray, Sir, do not throw away your thanks, before you know whether I have deſerv'd 'em or not. O! is that your deſign? Sir, you muſt not go in there.   [Petruchio *going to the door.*

Petr. How, Sir, not go in?

John. No, Sir, moſt certainly not go in.

Petr. She's my ſiſter, and I will ſpeak with her.

John. If ſhe were your mother, Sir, you ſhould not, though it were but to aſk her bleſſing.

Petr. Since you are ſo poſitive, I'll try.   [*Fight.*

John. You ſhall find me a man of my word, Sir.

2   *Duke.*

Duke. Nay, pray gentlemen, hold, let me com: pofe this matter ; why do you make a fcruple of letting us fee Conftantia ?

John. Why, Sir, 'twould turn a man's head round to hear thefe fellows talk fo ; there is not one word true of all that he has faíd.

Duke. Then you do not know where Con-ftantia is ?

John. Not I, by heavens.

Fred. O monftrous impudence ! upon my life; Sir, I faw him fhut her up into that houfe, and know his temper fo, that if I had not ftopp'd him, I darè fwear by this time he would have ravifh'd her.

John. Now that is two lies : for firft he did not fee her ; and next the lady I led in is not to be ravifh'd, fhe is fo willing.

Duke. But look you, Sir, this doubt may eafily be clear'd : let either Petruchio or I but fee her; and if fhe bè not Conftantia; we èngage our ho-nours (though wo fhould know her) never to dif-cover who fhe is.

John. Ay, but there's the point now, that I can ne'er confent to ?

Duke. Why ?

John. Becaufe I gave her my word to the contrary. *Duke:*

Duke. And did you never break your word with a woman ?

John. Never before I lay with her; and that's the cafe now.

Petr. Pifh, I won't be kept off thus any longer: Sir, either let me enter, or I'll force my way.

Fred. No, pray Sir, let that be my office, I will be reveng'd on him for having betray'd his friendfhip to me.

[Petr. *and* Fred. *offer to fight with* John.

Duke. Nay, you fhall not offer him foul play neither. Hold, brother, pray a word; and with you too, Sir.

John. Pox on't, would they would make an end of this bufinefs, that I might be with her again. Hark you, gentlemen, I'll make you a fair propofition; leave off this ceremony among yourfelves, and thofe difmal threats againft me; fillip up, crofs or pile who fhall begin firft, and I'll do the beft I can to entertain you all one after another.

Enter Antonio.

Ant. Now do my fingers itch to be about fome body's ears for the lofs of my gold. Ha! what's here to do, fword's drawn? I muft make one, though it coft me the finging of ten John Dory's

I more

more. · Courage, brave boy, I'll ftand by thee as long as this tool here lafts; and it was once a good one.

Petr. Who's this? Antonio! O, Sir, you are welcome, you fhall be e'en judge between us. ·

Ant. No, no, no, not I, Sir, thank ye; I'll make work for others to judge of, I'm refolv'd to fight.

Petr. But we won't fight with you.

Ant. Then put up your fwords, or by this hand I'll lay about me.

John. Well faid, old Bilbo, i'faith.

[*They put up their fwords.*

Petr. Pray hear us, tho'; this gentleman faw him lock up my fifter into that houfe, and he re- fufes to let us fee her.

Ant. How, friend, is this true?

John. Nay, good Sir, let not our friendfhip be broken before it is well made. Look ye, gentle- men, to fhew you that you are all miftaken, and that my formal friend there is an afs.-----

Fred. I thank you, Sir.

John. I'll give my confent that this gentleman here fhall fee her, if his information can fatisfy you.

                                            Duke.

Duke. Yes, yes ; he knows her very well.

John. Then, Sir, go in here if you pleafe ; I dare truft him with her, for he is too old to do her either good or harm,

Fred. I wonder how my Gentleman will get off from all this.

John. I fhall be even with you, Sir, another time, for all your grinning.

Enter a Servant.

How now ? where is he ?

Ser. He's run out o'the back door, Sir.

John. How fo ?

Ser. Why, Sir, he's run after the gentlewoman you brought in,

John. 'Sdeath, how durft you let her out ?

Ser. Why, Sir, I knew nothing.

John. No, thou ignorant rafcal, and therefore I'll beat fomething into thee,   [*Beats him.*

Fred. What, you won't kill him ?

John. Nay, come not near me, for if thou doft, by heavens I'll give thee as much ; and would do fo however, but that I won't lofe time from looking after my dear fweet------a pox confound you all.   [*Goes in and fhuts the door after him.*

Duke. What ? he has fhut the door.

Fred. It's no matter, I'll lead you to a private back way, by that corner, where we fhall meet him.   [*Exeunt.*

END OF THE FOURTH ACT.

ACT V.   SCENE I.

Enter Antonio's Servant, Conftables *and* Officers.

Ser. A Young woman, fay'ft thou, and her mother ?

Man. Yes, juft now come to the houfe. Not an hour ago.

Ser. It muft be they; here, friend, here's money for you; be fure you take 'em, and I'll reward you better when you have done.

Con. But neighbour, ho,--hup--fhall I now--hup --know thefe parties ? for I would--hup--execute my office--hup--like--hup--a fober perfon.

Man. That's hard: but you may eafily know the mother, for fhe is--hup--drunk.

Con. Nay--hup--if fhe be drunk, let--hup--me
                                        alone

alone to maul her; for--hup--I abhor a drunkard,
--let it be man--woman, or--hup--child.

Man. Ay; neighbour, one may fee you hate
drinking indeed.

Con. Why, neighbour--hup--did you ever fee
me drunk? anfwer me that queftion; did you
ever--hup--fee me drunk?

Man. No, never, never; come away, here's
the houfe.   [*Exeunt*

S C E N E II.

Enter firft Conftantia.

i Con. Oh, whither fhall I run to hide myfelf!
The conftable has feiz'd the landlady, and I'm
afraid the poor child too. How to return to Don
Frederick's houfe, I know not; and if I knew, I
durft not, after thofe things the landlady has told
me of him. If I get not from this drunken rabble,
I expofe my honour; and if I fall into my brother's hands, I lofe my life: ye powers above,
look down and help me; I am faulty, I confefs,
but greater faults have often met with lighter pu-
nifhments.

Then let not heavier yet on me be laid,
Be what I will, I'm ftill what you have made.

Q 2   *Enter*

Enter Don John.

John. I'm almoſt dead with running, and will be ſo quite, but I will overtake her.

1 *Con.* Hold, Don John, hold.

John. Who's that? Ha! is it you, my dear.

1 *Con.* For heaven's ſake, Sir, carry me from hence, or I'm utterly undone.

John. Phoo, pox, this is th' other; now could I almoſt beat her, for but making me the propoſition : Madam, there are ſome a-coming that will do it a great deal better; but I am in ſuch haſte that I vow to gad, madam------

1 *Con.* Nay, pray Sir, ſtay, Sir, you are concerned in this as well as I; for your woman is taken.

John. Ha! my woman?   [*Goes back to her.* I vow to gad, madam, I do ſo highly honour your ladyſhip, that I would venture my life a thouſand times to do you ſervice.   But pray where is ſhe?

1 *Con.* Why, Sir, ſhe is taken by the conſtable.

John. Conſtable! which way went he?

1 *Con.* I cannot tell, for I run out into the ſtreets juſt as he had ſeized upon your landlady.

John. Plague o' my landlady, I meant t'other woman.

1 *Con.*

1 *Con.* Other woman, Sir! I have feen no other woman ever fince I left your houfe.

John. 'Sheart, what have I been doing here then all this while? Madam, your moſt humble--

1 *Con.* Good Sir, be not ſo cruel, as to leave me in this diſtreſs.

John. No, no, no; I'm only going a little way, and will be back again prefently.

1 *Con.* But, pray Sir, hear me; I'm in that danger------

John. No, no, no; I vow to gad, madam, no danger in the world: Let me alone, I warrant you.   [*Exit.*

1 *Con.* He's gone, and I a loft, wretched, miſerable creature for ever.

Enter Antonio,

Ant. O, there fhe is.

1 *Con.* Who's this, Antonio? the fierceſt enemy I have.   [*Runs out.*

Ant. Are you ſo nimble-footed, gentlewoman? If I don't overtake you for all this, it ſhall go hard-- She'll break my wind with a pox to her. A plague confound all whores.   [*Exit.*

Q 3   SCENE

SCENE III.

Enter Mother *to the second* Conſtantia, *and* Kinſwoman.

Kinſ. But, madam, be not ſo angry, perhaps
ſhe'll come again.

Mo. O kinſwoman, never ſpeak of her more;
for ſhe's an odious creature, to leave me thus i' th'
lurch. I that have given her all her breeding,
and inſtructed her with my own principles of edu-
cation.

Kinſ. I proteſt, madam, I think ſhe's a perſon
that knows as much of all that as----

Mo. Knows, kinſwoman! There's ne'er a woman in Italy, of thrice her years, knows ſo much
the procedures of a true gallantry, and the infal-
lible principles of an honourable friendſhip as ſhe
does.

Kinſ. And therefore, madam, you ought to love
her.

Mo. No, fie upon her; nothing at all, as I am
a chriſtian: when once a perſon fails in funda-
mentals, ſhe's at a period with me. Beſides, with
all her wit, Conſtantia is but a fool, and calls all
the meniarderies of a bonne mien affectation.

Kinſ.

Kinf. Indeed I muſt confeſs, ſhe's given a little too much to the careleſs way.

Mo. Ay, there you have hit it, kinſwoman; the careleſs way has quite undone her. Will you believe me, kinſwoman? as I am a chriſtian, I never could make her do this, nor carry her body thus, but juſt when my eye was upon her: as ſoon as ever my back was turned, whip, her elbows were quite out again: Would not you ſtrange now at this?

Kinf. Bleſs me, ſweet goodneſs! But pray, madam, how came Conſtantia to fall out with your ladyſhip? Did ſhe take any thing ill of you?

Mo. As I'm a chriſtian I can't reſolve you, unleſs it were that I led the dance firſt; but for that ſhe muſt excuſe me; I know ſhe dances well, but there are others who perhaps underſtand the right ſwim of it as well as ſhe,

Enter Don Frederick,

And though I love Conſtantia----

Fred. How's this? Conſtantia?

Mo. I know no reaſon why I ſhould be debarr'd the privilege of ſhewing my own parts too ſometimes.

Fred.

Fred. If I am not miftaken that other woman is fhe Don John and I were directed to, when we came firft to town, to bring us acquainted with Conftantia : I'll try to get fome intelligence from her. Pray, lady, have I never feen you before ?

Kinf. Yes, Sir, I think you have, with another ftranger, a friend of yours, one day as I was coming out of the church.

Fred. I'm right then : And pray who were you talking of ?

Mo. Why, Sir, of an inconfiderate, inconfiderable perfon, that has at once both forfeited the honour of my concern, and the concern of her own honour.

Fred. Very fine indeed: And is all this intended for the beautiful Conftantia ?

Mo. O fie upon her, Sir, an odious creature, as I'm a chriftian, no beauty at all.

Fred. Why, does not your ladyfhip think her handfome ?

Mo. Serioufly, Sir, I don't think fhe's ugly, but as I am a chriftian, my pofition is, that no true beauty can be lodg'd in that creature, who is not in fome meafure buoy'd up with a juft fenfe of

what

what is incumbent to the devoir of a perſon of quality.

Fred. That poſition, madam, is a little ſevere, but however ſhe has been incumbent formerly, as your ladyſhip is pleas'd to ſay ; now that ſhe's married, and her huſband own's the child, ſhe is ſufficiently juſtified for all that ſhe has done.

Mo. Sir, I muſt bluſhingly beg leave to ſay, you are there in an error. I know there has been paſſages of love between 'em, but with a temperament ſo innocent, and ſo refin'd, as it did impoſe a negative upon the very poſſibility of her being with child.

Fred. Sure ſhe is not well acquainted with her. Pray, madam, how long have you known Conſtantia ?

Mo. Long enough, I think, Sir ; for I had the good fortune, or rather the ill one, to help her firſt to the light of the world.

Fred. Now cannot I diſcover, by the fineneſs of this dialect, whether ſhe be the mother or the midwife : I had beſt aſk t'other woman.

Mo. No, Sir, I aſſure you, my daughter Conſtantia has never had a child : A child ! ha, ha, ha ! O goodneſs ſave us, a child !

Fred.

Fred. O, then she is the mother, and, it seems, is not informed of the matter. Well, madam, I shall not dispute this with you any farther; but give me leave to wait upon your daughter; for her friend, I assure you, is in great impatience to see her.

Mo. Friend, Sir? I know none she has? I'm sure she loaths the very sight of him.

Fred. Of whom?

Mo. Why, of Antonio, Sir, he that you were pleas'd to say had got my daughter with child, Sir, ha---ha---ha---

Fred. Still worse and worse; 'Slife cannot she be content with not letting me understand her, but must also resolve obstinately not to understand me, because I speak plain? Why, madam, I cannot express myself your way, therefore be not offended at me for it; I tell you I do not know Antonio, nor ever named him to you: I to'd you that the Duke has own'd Constantia for his wife, that her brother and he are friends, and are both now in search after her.

Mo. Then, as I'm a christian, I suspect we have both been equally involved in the misfortune of a mistake. Sir, I am in the derniere confusion

to

to avow, that, though my daughter Conſtantia has been liable to ſeveral addreſſes, yet ſhe never has had the honour to be produc'd to his grace.

Fred. So then you put her to bed to----

Mo. Antonio, Sir, one whom my ebb of fortune forc'd me to enter into a negotiation with, in reference to my daughter's perſon; but, as I am a chriſtian, with that candor in the aꞓtion, as I was in no kind deny'd to be a witneſs of the thing.

Fred. So, now the thing is out: this is a damn'd bawd, and I as damn'd a rogue for what I did to Don John: for o'my conſcience, this is that Conſtantia the fellow told me of. I'll make him amends whate'er it coſt me. Lady, you muſt give me leave not to part with you, till you meet with your daughter, for ſome reaſons I ſhall tell you hereafter.

Mo. Sir, I am ſo highly your obligee for the manner of your enquiries, and you have grounded your determinations upon ſo juſt a baſis, that I ſhall not be aſham'd to own myſelf a votary to all your commands. [*Exeunt.*

SCENE

S C E N E   IV.

Enter second Conftantia.

2 *Con.* So I'm once more freed from Antonio;
but whither to go now, that's the queftion; nothing troubles me, but that he was fent up by that
young fellow, for I lik'd him with my foul, would
he had lik'd me fo too.

Enter Don John *and a* Shop-keeper.

John. Which way went fhe?

Shop. Who?

John. The woman.

Shop. What woman?

John. Why, a young woman, a handfome woman, the handfomeft woman thou ever faw'ft in
thy life: Speak quickly, Sirrah, or thou fhalt
fpeak no more.

Shop. Why, yonder's a woman; what a devil
ails this fellow?   [*Exit.*

John. O my dear foul, take pity o' me, and
give me comfort, for I'm e'en dead for want of
thee.

2 *Con.* O, you're a fine gentleman indeed, to
fhut me up in your houfe, and fend another man
to me.

John.

John. Pray hear me.

2 *Con.* No, I will never hear you more after fuch an injury ; what would you have done, if I had been kind to you, that could ufe me thus before ?

John. By my troth that's fhrewdly urg'd.

2 *Con.* Befides, you bafely broke your word.

John. But will you hear nothing? nor did you bear nothing? I had three men upon me at once, and had I not confented to let that old fellow up, who came to my refcue, they had all broken in whether I would or no.

2 *Con.* Faith, it may be it was fo, for I remember I heard a noife; but, fuppofe it was not fo, what then? Why, then I'll love him however. Hark you, Sir, I ought now to ufe you very fcurvily, but I can't find in my heart to do it.

John. Then God's bleffing on thy heart for it.

2 *Con.* But a---

John. What?

2 *Con.* I would fain----

John. Ay, fo would I ; come let's go.

2 *Con.* I would fain know whether you can be kind to me.

John. That thou fhalt prefently : come away.

2 *Con.*

2 Con. And will you always?

John. Always? I can't fay fo; but I will as often as I can.

2 Con. Phoo, I mean love me:

John. Well, I mean that too.

2 Con. Swear then.

John. That I will upon my knees : What fhall I fay?

2 Con. Nay, ufe what words you pleafe, fo they be but hearty, and not thofe that are fpoken by the prieft, for that charm feldom proves fortu-nate.

John. I fwear, then, by thy fair felf, that look'ft fo like a deity, and art the only thing I now can think of, that I'll adore thee to my dying day.

2 Con. And here I'll vow, the minute thou doft leave me, I'll leave the world, that's kill myfelf.

John. O my dear heavenly creature !----

[*Kiffes her.*

That kifs now has almoft put me into a fwoon: for heaven's fake let's quickly out of the ftreets, for fear of another fcuffle. I durft encounter a whole army for thy fake; but yet, methinks, I had better try my courage another way; what think'ft thou?

2 Con.

2 Con. Well, well, why don't you then ?

[*As they are going out, enter firſt Conſtantia, and juſt then Antonio ſeizes
upon her.*

John. Who's this, my old new friend has got
there ?

Ant. O, have I caught you gentlewoman at laſt?
Come, give me my gold.

1 Con. I hope he takes me for another, I won't
anſwer, for I had rather he ſhould take me for
any one than who I am.

John. Pray, Sir, who is that you have there by
the hand ?

Ant. A perſon of honour, Sir, that has broke
open my trunks, and run away with all my gold ;
yet I'll hold ten pound I'll have it whip'd out of
her again.

2 Con. Done, I'll hold you ten pounds of that
now.

Ant. Ha! by my troth you have reaſon ; and,
lady, I aſk your pardon ; but I'll have it whipp'd
out of you then, goſſip.

John. Hold, Sir, you muſt not meddle with my
goods.

Ant. Your goods! how came ſhe to be yours ?
I'm

I'm fure I bought her of her mother for five hundred good pieces of gold, and fhe was a-bed with me all night too; deny that if you dare.

2 Con. Well, and what did you do when I was a-bed with you all night? confefs that if you dare.

Ant. Umph, fay you fo?

1 Con. I'll try if this lady will help me, for I know not whether elfe to go.

Ant. I fhall be afham'd I fee utterly, except I make her hold her tongue. Pray, Sir, by your leave, I hope you will allow me the fpeech of one word with your goods here, as you call her; 'tis but a fmall requeft.

John. Ay, Sir, with all my heart. How, Conftantia! Madam, now you have feen that lady, I hope you will pardon the hafte you met me in a little while ago; if I committed a fault, you muft thank her for it.

1 Con. Sir, if you will, for her fake, be perfuaded to protect me from the violence of my brother, I fhall have reafon to thank you both.

John. Nay, madam, now that I am in my wits again, and my heart's at eafe, it fhall go very hard but I will fee yours fo too; I was before diftracted,

ſtracted, and it is not ſtrange the love of her
ſhould hinder me from remembring what was due
to you, ſince it made me forget myſelf.

1 *Con.* Sir, I do know too well the power of
love, by my own experience, not to pardon all
the effects of it in another.

Ant. Well, then, I promiſe you, if you will but
help me to my gold again, (I mean that which
you and your mother ſtole out of my trunk) that
I'll never trouble you more.

2 *Con.* A match; and 'tis the beſt that you and
I could ever make.

John. Pray, madam, fear nothing; by my love
I'll ſtand by you, and ſee that your brother ſhall
do you no harm.

2 *Con.* Hark you, Sir, a word; how dare you
talk of love, or ſtanding by any lady but me, Sir.

John. By my troth that was a fault; but I did
not mean in your way; I meant it only civilly.

2 *Con.* Ay, but if you are ſo very civil a gentleman, we ſhall not be long friends: I ſcorn to ſhare
your love with any one whatſoever; and for my
part, I'm reſolv'd either to have all or nothing.

John. Well, my dear little rogue, thou ſhalt

have it all prefently, as foon as we can but get rid
of this company.

2 *Con.* Phoo, you are always abufing me.

Enter Frederick *and* Mother.

Fred. Come now, madam, let not us fpeak one
word more, but go quietly about our bufinefs;
not but that I think it the greateft pleafure in the
world to hear you talk, but----

Mo. Do you indeed, Sir? I fwear then, good
wits jump, Sir; for I have thought fo myfelf a
very great while.

Fred. You've all the reafon imaginable. O!
Don John, I afk thy pardon: but I hope I fhall
make thee amends, for I have found out the mother, and fhe has promifed me to help thee to thy
miftrefs again.

John. Sir, you may fave your labour, the bufinefs is done, and I am fully fatisfied.

Fred. And doft thou know who fhe is?

John. No faith, I never afk'd her name.

Fred. Why then, I'll make thee yet more fatisfy'd: this lady here is that very Conftantia----

John. Ha! thou haft not a-mind to be knock'd
o'er the pate too, haft thou?

Fred.

Fred. No, Sir, nor dare you do it neither ; but for certain this is that very felf-fame Conftantia that thou and I fo long look'd after.

John. I thought fhe was fomething more than ordinary ; but fhall I tell thee now a ftranger thing than all this ?

Fred. What's that ?

John. Why, I will never more touch any other woman for her fake.

Fred. Well, I fubmit that indeed is ftranger.

2 Con. Come, mother, deliver your purfe ; I have deliver'd myfelf up to this young fellow, and the bargain's made with that old fellow, fo he may have his gold again, that all fhall be well.

Mo. As I'm a chriftian, Sir, I took it away only to have the honour of reftoring it again ; for, my hard fate having not beftow'd upon me a fund which might capacitate me to make you prefents of my own, I had no way left for the exercife of my generofity, but by putting myfelf into a condition of giving back what was yours.

Ant. A very generous defign indeed. So, now I'll e'en turn a fober perfon, and leave off this wenching, and this fighting, for I begin to find it does not agree with me.

Fred,

Fred. Madam, I am heartily glad to meet your ladyſhip here ; we have been in very great diſorder ſince we ſaw you :---What's here, our landlady and the child again ?

Enter Duke, Petruchio, *and* Landlady, *with the child.*

Pet. Yes, we met her going to be whipp'd, in a drunken conſtable's hands, that took her for another.

John. Why, then, pray let her e'en be taken, and whipp'd for herſelf, for on my word ſhe deſerves it.

Land. Yes, I'm ſure of your good word at any time.

1 *Con.* Hark ye, dear landlady.

Land. O ſweet goodneſs ! is it you ? I have been in ſuch a peck of troubles ſince I ſaw you, they took me, and they tumbled me, and they haul'd me, and they pull'd me, and they call'd me painted Jezebel, and the poor little babe here did ſo take on. Come hither, my lord, come hither ; here is Conſtantia.

1 *Con.*

1 *Con.* For heaven's fake, peace ; yonder's my brother, and, if he difcovers me, I'm certainly ruin'd.

Duke. No, madam, there's no danger.

1 *Con.* Were there a thoufand dangers in thóſe arms, I would run thus to meet them.

Duke. O my dear! it were not fafe that any fhould be here at prefent ; for now my heart is fo o'erprefs'd with joy, that I fhould fcarce be able to defend thee.

Petr. Sifter, I'm fo afham'd of all the faults, which my miftake has made me guilty of, that I know not how to afk your pardon for them.

1 *Con.* No, brother, the fault was mine, in miftaking you fo much, as not to impart the whole truth to you at firft ; but having begun my love without your confent, I never durft acquaint you with the progrefs of it.

Duke. Come, let the confummation of our prefent joys blot out the memory of all thefe paft miftakes. ◄

John. And when fhall we confummate our joys ?

2 *Con.*

2 *Con.* Never:

We'll find out ways fhall make 'em laft for ever.

    John. Now fee the odds, 'twixt married folks
      and friends;

Our love begins juft where their paffion ends.

E P I.

EPILOGUE.

PErhaps you, gentlemen, expect to-day
The author of this fag end of a play,
According to the modern way of wit,
Should ftrive to be before-hand with the pit;
Begin to rail at you, and fubtly to
Prevent th' affront by giving the firft blow.
He wants not precedents, which often fway
In matters far more weighty than a play:
But he, no grave admirer of a rule,
Won't by example learn to play the fool.
The end of plays fhould be to entertain,
And not to keep the auditors in pain.
Giving our price, and for what trafh we pleafe,
He thinks, the play being done, you fhould have
    eafe.
No wit, no fenfe, no freedom, and a box,
Is much like paying money for the ftocks.
Befides, the author dreads the ftrut and mien
Of new-prais'd poets, having often feen
Some of his fellows, who have writ before,
When *Nell* has danc'd her jig, fteal to the door,
Hear the pit clap, and with conceit of that
Swell, and believe themfelves the Lord knows
    what.

Moft

Moſt writers now a-days are grown ſo vain,
That, once approv'd, they write, and write again ;
Till they have writ away the fame they got :
Our friend this way of writing fancies not ;
And hopes you will not tempt him with your
     praiſe,
To rank himſelf with ſome, that write new plays :
For he knows ways enough to be undone,
Without the help of poetry for one.

www.ingramcontent.com/pod-product-compliance
Lightning Source LLC
Chambersburg PA
CBHW021043030726
47496CB00006B/1664